The World of the Moho

Tyree Campbell

WolfSinger Publications ⟨ Brackettville, Texas

Dedicated and with gratitude to Edgar Rice Burroughs.
Thanks for all the adventures.

001: The Moho

The workers noticed him because he was a white man. He did not appear to be lost or wandering, but he was circling the opening to the Mandela Mine, now abandoned this past decade. At one point the mine had represented the economic hope of the South African government. Assured both gold and diamonds would be found in the depths of the Earth's crust. Unfortunately, neither eventuality proved out. Now there were workers half a mile away, exploiting the older De Beers Mine with the same hopes that fed the excavation of the Mandela, albeit with a little more success.

His name was Aldon McIntyre, he answered with mild annoyance to Allie, and he was twenty-nine years old. On the verge of a zero year, when men have been known to do the unexpected and even the off-beat—divorce or an abrupt change of employment, among others—he had taken leave from his job as a water quality expert for the state of Iowa to engage in his pastime, which was geology. He had a varied experience in outdoor activities—including SCUBA diving and spelunking. He knew his way around, but he was hardly an expert. An affection for nature and an attendant curiosity led him to explore.

Allie had an active outdoors physique; six foot two and wiry, with a tan adequate to the sunlight of South Africa. To prevent his dark brown hair from blocking his vision at a critical moment, he kept it short, not quite enough to comb. He had attired himself for heat and roughness: sturdy black boots, light blue work denims, and a gray gym shirt with the sleeves torn off just below the deltoids. A camouflage bush hat kept the sun off his head. Still, to a stranger and even to a few of those who knew him, he might have been anyone, a nondescript pedestrian on the crowded path of life. Even the workers returned to their duties, for he was clearly interested in a cause they had long ago given up for dead.

The electricity was still on at the mineshaft; the lights in the office declared this to be so. He stood midway between the cargo elevator that deposited workers and equipment almost three miles below and the blue-and-rust rental car with his backpack, pickax, and two hundred yards of coiled yellow nylon rope. Here he hesitated: there might be no coming back from what he was about to do. He might easily turn around and drive back to Johannesburg with no one the wiser to his lack of heart; he had simply wanted to get away for a while. He thought about that for a few moments, until perspiration began to bead on his forehead. That decided him; he had after all come this far.

With the backpack situated, the pickax dangled from his canvass equipment belt along with a Swiss army knife, a battery-powered flashlight, and two filled canteens of dark green plastic. With coils of rope looped over his left shoulder, Allie headed for the elevator and the buttons that controlled it. He was just about to step aboard when the peremptory demand reached his ears.

"*Wat maak jy?*"

He paused and turned around.

She was chestnut-brown with eyes like anthracite, and she was dressed in miner's garb: loose-fitting, pale turquoise pullover and rugged blue denims that looked as if they had been in a store not two days ago, and scuffed, brown hiking boots. Despite the work attire, she was no miner. Her fine black hair was loose and just a little dusty; for a miner, it should have been shorter, to avoid inadvertent tangles with equipment that could snap her neck. She carried herself fully erect, and might have been a descendant of the great Cetewayo, whose Zulu army had slaughtered the British at Isandlwana almost 150 years earlier. She had that kind of demeanor. Fists on hips, she was almost, but not quite, hostile, needing only a spark to set her off.

Allie shook his head. He recognized the language as Afrikaans, but he spoke only a few words of Dutch, the most important enabling him to locate the toilet and to purchase another beer. "*Ik ben een Amerikaan,*" he tried, with a poor accent.

Taking a couple steps closer, she switched to Queen's English, with a very faint Cockney flavor to it. "I asked you what the bloody hell you were doing," she snapped. "This mine is closed."

"Yes, I know."

"You have to leave here."

"Who are you?" he asked.

The question seemed irrelevant to her. "My name is Thadie Mayane," she growled. "More important, however, is my title. I am the Assistant Site Forewoman. Now, get back into your vehicle and leave this area. You have no business here."

Allie closed to within a pace of her and handed her a business card, which she reluctantly accepted. At this distance, he saw she came within two or three inches of his height, but her fierce attitude made her appear taller.

"Aldon McIntyre?" she read aloud. "Water Quality Testing?" She tossed the card back at him; it fluttered to the ground. Ironic laughter colored her tone. "There's no bloody water here. Look around you. Do you see any water?"

"It could be subterranean."

Her black eyebrows rutted, and her voice dropped half an octave. "What?"

"It might be underground."

Her thin lips twisted in the rictus of a snarl. "I bloody well know what 'subterranean' means."

Without taking his eyes from her, Allie bent and retrieved the card. "I want to take some samples from the shaft," he explained—a lie, of course, but she would not know that. "If there was once water in the ground, it might be brought back under certain conditions, and wells might be dug to bring it up. That might change the land, don't you think?"

"*Umbhedo,*" she muttered.

He did not speak a word of Zulu, but the tone in which she uttered the word left no doubt as to its meaning. *Yeah, well, I didn't believe it, either*, he thought.

Still, she temporized, just a little, and cleaned up her language.

"At the bottom of the mine, they were digging a spur, a horizontal tunnel," she said. "They ran into a vein of quartz. The floor of that tunnel gave way, and there was some damage to the lower shaft. Fortunately, no work was being done down there at the time. Inspectors went down to assess the damage. It was decided to close the mine and cut the losses of the investment. Nobody has been down there since. That was—"

"Almost two years ago," he said. "I did some research."

Her response bit. "Of course you did."

"I'm going down," he insisted.

She turned her face away and spat her words at the dusty ground. "Shit," she hissed. "Shit, shit, shit." After blowing a sigh, she raised her face again. "I reckon I can't stop you without a fight," she said. "And by the time the police get here, if they come out at all, you'll already be all the way down. So all right. I know the mine. I worked it when I first started here. I'll go with you. Just…just don't touch anything. I'll operate the lift."

"Fair enough."

"A word of caution, *Meneer* McIntyre. I have a black belt in jiu-jitsu. If you…try anything, you'll be left down there, and not in very good condition."

He stuck with the lie. "All I want to do is take some samples from the mineshaft walls, *Mej* Mayane."

They boarded the lift, and she pushed the correct two green buttons. Power kicked in immediately, and they began to descend, slowly at first, before gradually picking up speed. Machinery whined and rasped unnervingly, and Allie felt as if he were poised on the edge of a precipice, which in a manner of speaking, he was. Two strings of lights along the shaft lit their way. Already the heat gradient stifled the air. Where he was struggling to breathe, she scarcely seemed to notice the temperature.

"You know it's over four kilometers down," she hinted, still testing his resolve.

"Which means it will be warmer by about sixty degrees Celsius," he added, and finished disingenuously, "Which is why I only need to go down a mile or so."

She frowned, thoughtful. "So you don't know?"

"What's that?"

"The measurements are in metric," she told him, with mock patience, as if he should have known. "Temperature increases by about twenty-five degrees Celsius for every kilometer of depth. During the excavations, we had a cooling system so people could work. Even so, we…lost a few. But the point is, once you go below about two kilometers—not quite a mile and a half—the temperature starts to go down, not up. It's around thirty-five to forty degrees Celsius at the bottom."

"Which is what, a hundred and five or so in Fahrenheit?"

Mayane shrugged. "About that, I reckon."

"That's…unlikely," Allie said, puzzled.

She turned to stare at him. "*Meneer* McIntyre, are you calling me—"

"No," he hastened to say. "No, not at all. It just seems…"

She softened. "It does. And I agree. But it is true."

"Then let's go all the way to the bottom," he said, masking his relief in a casual tone. Now he could abandon part of the lie. "The further down we go, the more reliable my samples should be." He gave her a sidelong look, and decided to relieve the tedium with a conversation, if she would cooperate. "You said you started out in this mine?"

Mayane answered readily enough. "When I was sixteen," she replied. "Six hour shifts daily, six hours of school five days a week. I managed to save a little even after I gave half my earnings to my parents. The savings, plus a scholarship to the University of Zululand, plus a lot of sweat here, led to three promotions. When the Site Foreman retires, in about five years, I have a shot at that position."

She fell silent, and did not ask to know anything of him. The lift lurched a little, startling them both, but it quickly recovered.

"Ghosts," he said.

Under her dark skin, she blanched. She flashed at him a stricken look. "Don't say that!"

He quickly apologized, adding, "I don't understand."

She spoke barely above a whisper. "All mineshafts are the abodes of those who have died in them."

Allie decided not to challenge her belief. Doubtless it was intensely tribal. He tried to change the subject.

"I've loved caves and caverns and mineshafts ever since I was a little boy. But I rarely got to see any. We moved around a lot. When I finally went off to college, I majored in organic chemistry at the behest of my father, but I snuck in a minor in geology, which was my first love. Unfortunately, there were few opportunities for me in either field—and my grades were not good enough to get me into—"

The lift lurched again, and this time it trembled, as if something above it were about to come loose.

"It's all right," Mayane said, not very convincingly. "This some-times happens."

"It's a good thing you're here," he said. "After this one, I would have panicked."

She gazed out at the passing mineshaft. "What makes you think I'm not?" she asked.

That, more than the behavior of the machinery, shook Allie.

This was her territory. If she was concerned about it, what did that bode for him? Once again he wondered whether he should have turned back while he still had the chance. With metal groaning above him, he had to consider the age and maintenance of the equipment. Still, Mayane had thought it safe enough to descend; that had to count for something.

Allie dabbed at his forehead with a handkerchief. "How far down are we now?" he asked her.

Still peering out and down, she gave a light shrug. "We just passed the marker for one and a half kilometers."

He tried a shaky grin. "I'm looking forward to that temperature drop."

Her hair fluttered. "Do you feel that?" she asked.

"A very light breeze," he said. "Almost imperceptible."

She gnawed an incisor at her lower lip. "There shouldn't be *any* bloody breeze. We're descending at the rate of six kilometers an hour. That won't send air through this screen."

Mayane leaned forward to take a better look below. In that moment, the lift shook again, and she stumbled. Before she could right herself, Allie caught her and held her up. He was going to wait until she had set her feet, but she said, icily, "You can let go of me, *Meneer.*"

Allie withdrew himself swiftly, and raised his hands in defense. "Sorry," he said. "I didn't…"

Ignoring him now, she leaned forward once more and looked down. Keeping his distance, Allie joined her at the lift door and followed her eyes. He had no idea what she was looking for or what she was seeing below. He himself saw only a darkness poorly lit by the two strings of lights.

"Anything?" he asked.

The sound of his voice intruded into an uneasy silence. She did not look at him, nor did she respond. Neither did she slow the lift. He stepped back to the rear of the lift and left her alone with her worries. Despite leaning, her spine was rigid, a harsh response to his touch. His lips puffed out with his sigh. He had only meant to prevent her from falling.

White man, he thought, and black woman. Time had made the chasm too wide to cross. Although he had meant nothing untoward in saving her from falling, he was confronting an ingrained hostility born of centuries of oppression. He had not come to South Africa to ease that hostility, but it had reared its ugly head outside in the dust and here in the lift, and there was nothing he would be allowed to do about it.

"What are you looking for?" he tried.

She did not turn around. "I'm looking for anything that would explain this breeze," she replied. "It's growing stronger. Can't you feel it?"

"Not back here, no. What does the air smell like?"

She tested it with an audible sniff. "I-I'm not sure."

That uncertainty, too, scared him. If she, the expert, did not know…

"Decay, decomposition, peaches?"

Mayane barked a laugh. Her shoulders trembled. "P-peaches?" She turned back around. "You said *peaches?*"

Allie spread his hands helplessly. "I don't know, pick a smell."

She considered. "There is a very slight fruity scent to it."

"Somebody's spoiled lunch?"

"No. I told you, no one was down there when the floor of the spur collapsed. *Ergo*, no lunch."

"Ergo?"

"It's Latin for 'therefore.'"

"I bloody well know what it means," he snapped.

Shocked momentarily, she burst into a full-bodied laugh. After it waned, she said, "I guess I've asked for that. Look, I'm sorry. You meant no harm. It's just that…well…"

"I think I understand."

"I think maybe you do, at that." A marker passed upwards. "Two kilometers," she announced.

"Halfway there."

Once more the uneasy silence returned. Allie no longer concerned himself with it. Although he was sweating profusely now, the temperature seemed to be dropping, just as she had said. It might have been his imagination; he hoped not. A hundred degrees was just a number; the heat it represented was daunting. His skin began to cool, ever so slightly. He did not question how that could be, but accepted it gratefully.

"Two and a half," she said.

The temperature definitely was falling. She did not say I told you so. Taking a chance, he joined her at the door, once more at arm's length. Now the breeze, though very warm, chilled him, for the skin of his face was still moist. He could not help but notice Mayane's face barely had a sheen to it. He decided not to comment; there were enough differences between them.

"Three kilometers."

This time, Allie saw the marker pass upwards. Its disappearance above made it seem so final. His heart began a slow but steady rate increase as the lift descended further and further into the depths. Mayane continued to stare down into the shaft; he himself saw little of interest. The strings of light stretched as far down as he could see. But the breeze, if anything, was a little stronger.

"Three and a half kilometers," Mayane said moving back to the control panel to slow the lift. As if to ease his concern, she added, "The lift will stop automatically when we reach the bottom of the shaft."

You hope, he thought. But he said nothing aloud. He tried to estimate the meters now, regarding them as the more familiar unit of measure called yards. The lift continued to decelerate. The sweet scent grew stronger, as did the breeze. Mayane, back at her post by the door, resumed her vigil.

Allie, belatedly, wondered why she had slowed the lift if it was going to come to a stop at the bottom anyway. After a moment he asked the question.

"There might have been another cave-in or rock collapse," she explained, without looking up. "That's why I'm also watching now."

She had succeeded in giving him one more thing to worry about. He moved in beside her to watch, too.

Gradually a cluster of boulders and chunks of rubble came into view some fifty yards further down. When Allie pointed, Mayane said, "That was there before. It won't impact the lift."

Metal screeched and protested as the brakes slowed the lift's progress. It came to a stop not a foot from the uppermost boulder. Allie drew several shallow breaths and exhaled each one in a burst of air. Mayane raised the door and stepped out onto the boulder.

"Coming?" she said sharply, as if she did not have all day to indulge him.

The lights continued to function, and Allie noticed a string of them leading along the ceiling of the tunnel off to the right of the lift. A brief calculation told him the direction was roughly to the west. He settled the backpack across his shoulders, looped the rope, and gingerly followed her down the pile of detritus to the tunnel, the flashlight in his hand showing the way.

Here the breeze was enough to ruffle Mayane's hair and waft in against his chest through his shirt sleeves. The lights and the flashlight failed to illuminate clearly what lay ahead, only that the tunnel continued for some distance. Even so, they moved cautiously, uncertain of the footing. At several spots they were forced to wind their way around fallen rocks and timbers. Allie glanced up from time to time, wondering whether the tunnel ceiling would hold. He heard the hiss of loose dirt falling, like sand in a giant hourglass. The sound of it echoed in the tunnel, as if the surrounding rock had itself become a ghost.

"Up ahead," Mayane said pointing to a blackness where the lights had failed. "There's the blockage. And this is as good a place as any to take your samples."

"What's on the other side of that cave-in?" he asked.

"I don't know," she said irritably. "I've never been that far. I've never even been this bloody far. Take your bloody samples!"

He passed her and continued on his way, the flashlight marking his progress.

"What the bloody hell are you *doing*?" she called. Her voice, like the falling dirt, echoed.

"I want to see if there is a way past."

Mayane heaved an exasperated sigh and her words had a sarcastic bite to them. "I thought you came here to take samples," she said, following him. "You're not here for that. You lied to me."

"I didn't expect anyone to come with me," he muttered.

She gave him a hard shove. "Damn you."

Recovering, he began to climb the rocks of the cave-in. It appeared to him, in the light from the flashlight, that there was an opening atop the pile. A very dim light was shining through it from the other side. Here, too, the breeze was powerful enough to blow dust into his eyes. He paused to unzip a pocket in the backpack and removed a pair of goggles. After a brief hesitation, he dug out a spare pair and offered it to Mayane, who snatched it angrily from his hand.

"Would you mind telling me what you *did come* here for?" she asked, with forced calm.

"The Moho," he told her.

"The...what?"

With a sigh he stopped just below the top of the pile. Wind blew through his hair. "The Mohorovičić discontinuity. You *have* heard of it?"

"Don't be bloody stupid, *of course* I have. But we're, I don't know, ten or fifteen miles above it."

"I'm not so sure."

Looking up at him, she planted fists on her hips. "And why not?"

Allie sat on a boulder and turned around to face her. The dim light cast his face in shadows. "I read the official report on the cave-in, in an obscure journal called *World Geology Today*. The remark about the breeze down here intrigued me. Nobody else placed any significance to it but given the floor of the tunnel had collapsed, I had to wonder whether there was a way into the Earth."

"Jules Verne," she sneered. "Good fiction, but mostly bad movies."

He nodded. "Yeah."

"That explains the rope," she said, ice in her tone now. "I should have known something was amiss. I was so focused on getting rid of you..."

"Send the lift back down after you get back up there," he said. "If you would, please."

She frowned. "What are you going to do?"

"That depends on what's on the other side of this cave-in. If the floor collapsed there, it may be worth investigating."

"For an article in *World Geology Today*, I suppose," she said derisively.

He ignored her tone. "That would be nice," he said. "But first, I'd have to have something to base it on. Thank you for all your help, *Mej* Mayane." He turned and began crawling toward the opening.

The opening gave way to a rugged passageway of shattered rock. The going made Allie wish he had worn sturdier gloves. Ahead, the light was stronger, although it still seemed to come from a distance. Sweat crept under his goggles, and dust sifted into his nostrils. It was the light that drove him forward; had it not been present, he might have abandoned the attempt altogether. But the light simply did not belong there, and it had to come from somewhere.

The "Wait" surprised him, and he paused in mid-crawl to glance back. God only knew why, but Thadie Mayane was coming along, too. She looked too determined to be dissuaded from following him …no, from accompanying him. He flashed the flashlight at her face. Her dark skin glistened with the brighter light. Before she could protest, he turned the light away.

"What the hell is it with you?" he growled. "I thought you'd be pleased to be well rid of me."

She coughed in the dust. "People saw us come down here," she said, fighting a dry throat. "If I go back up without you, I'd have paperwork in three bloody copies in each of six different bloody languages to fill out." She made a little motion with her hand. "Go on, get going. It's tight enough in here as it is."

Head shaking, Allie moved on. The rubble gave way to a slope that yielded under his weight, slowing his progress. Twice Mayane shoved the soles of his boots to hurry him on. Twenty yards ahead yawned a light-filled chasm where the floor had collapsed. His world was now filled with things that should not be. His heart began to race, and a blend of anticipation and fear formed a lump in his throat. Down the slope, he encountered blocks of granite that had to be climbed over before he could reach the floor of the tunnel.

By this time, Mayane had caught him up. Slick with sweat, their arms collided as they reached to pull themselves over a flat boulder. "Does it seem cooler in here to you?" he asked.

"Oh, yes indeed, a good degree and a half cooler."

They shared a laugh and pushed on down the rubble. Soon enough, they were able to stand and walk. Cautiously they approached the opening—step, pause, step, pause. Eddies of air cooled them, and dried their skin, although it did little for their clothing.

"I don't know that I'd get much closer, *Meneer*," she said. "There's no telling how stable this spur is."

"I know," he replied. "But I have to see."

With his next step, the tunnel floor under them gave way.

002: Oh, Shit!

The immediate effect of the collapse was to knock both Allie and Mayane off their feet. Flat now against a great chunk of the floor, they found themselves hurtling down and at an angle into what appeared to be an abyss. Too frightened initially to get their bearings, they could but scream in terror. From time to time the slab of granite came to a stop, its passing blocked by an outcrop or a huge boulder. Other, smaller boulders, debris from the collapse, rolled past them and on down the great slope…or rolled or bounced over the slab, forcing them to dodge aside. Broken rock ground under the weight of the slab.

At one point, an abrupt halt to the slab's progress caused Allie to spill over the leading edge of the granite. Hanging on for dear life with one hand as bits of detritus bounded past him, he feared the end. The slab slipped, and threatened to pass over him, crushing him. A strong hand snagged his wrist and held him in place. In that moment, the slab broke down its barrier and continued to slide, rather like a snowboard, down the rugged slope.

"Kick," Mayane yelled.

Allie fought the front of the granite for a foothold and found a precarious one. It would have to do. His knee ached as he pushed his booted foot against the protruding rock. He started to reach up with his free hand, only to realize he was still holding the flashlight. How he had managed to save it, he had no idea. He looked up. There was her face, now the face of a guardian angel, a sight welcome to his heart and his spirit. She was holding onto his wrist with both hands now. Her feet had found a purchase on the surface of the slab as it continued to bound down the slope.

He tossed the flashlight up onto the rock and hoped it would not be lost. Anchoring his freed hand, he kicked against the front of the rock, shoving himself upward. Still holding his wrist, Mayane fell back, sitting now as she tugged mightily on his arm. Her dark face contorted with the strain of her efforts. He felt as if his shoulder socket were hollow now, and about to surrender to those efforts. Another kick brought him halfway onto the slab, so that only his legs dangled over the leading edge.

The slab struck a tree and uprooted it. The impact spilled him back over the edge. His weight threatened to take Mayane with him and end them both. The thought flashed through his mind that without him she might stand a fighting chance of survival. As if she was reading his mind, she denied him a suicide. With her feet under her now, she straightened her legs, pulling him up onto the slab. Her chest heaved; her body relieved at last of its burden.

The slab slowed, yawed a little, and continued down the slope. The rest of the avalanche passed on either side of them, including fragments of what appeared to be the lift. Allie and Mayane fell back onto the granite, gasping the warm but now humid air that refused to enter their lungs quickly enough. Allie seemed to recover first.

"Hold the air inside you for a beat," he told her, between breaths. She barely had the strength to stare at him, puzzled as she gasped, a bloody-do-*what?* expression on her face.

Even the effort of speaking cost him precious air. Following his own advice, he gradually caught his breath and crabbed across the rock to her. "Thadie," he cried, nudging her. "Hold each breath for a second or two, then exhale and take another one. Like this," he finished, and showed her what he meant.

Mayane seemed to understand. The slab bounced on something and caromed off to the left before continuing its downward track. She slipped a little, and this time he caught her.

"I've got you," he gasped, drawing her back toward the center of the slab. "I've got you."

For just a moment as they stabilized, her forehead pressed against his arm in relief and gratitude. Then, as if aware of what she had just done, she scrabbled away from him, dark eyes wild and wary. Her respiration was still ragged, made even more so by her moment of weakness. The slab twisted again and spilled her over onto her side. Again Allie reached out for her, but this time she slapped his hand away.

The slab slowed to a crawl. They had reached a flat area in the slope. Drawing slow, deep breaths now, they managed to sit up.

"This," he gasped, and hoped, "is about as far as we go."

She could only nod.

Presently they began to take in their surroundings. The shock of finding themselves in another world overwhelmed them. Mayane's hand pressed against her heart; Allie's mind blanked, taking in everything around him without identifying it. Finally, in self-defense, they both closed their eyes.

A minute passed. "Are you seeing this?" he breathed.

"Not...at the moment."

He opened his eyes.

Overhead, as far as the eye could see in any direction, a vaulted ceiling glowed with a faint white light that illuminated everything without revealing its source. It seemed to be emitted from massive clear crystals of quartz, and Allie recalled Mayane had told him the excavators had run into a vein of that mineral. Just below the ceiling, mist was gathering into wisps of clouds.

If that light was inexplicable, the terrain under it was even more so. A long but gentle slope extended from the collapsed mine far above down to a river valley with fields on the far side and trees—or tree-like growths—on the near side. Near the riverbank—Allie could not see on which side—rose a metal dish, rather like a radio astronomy telescope. He tended not to believe his eyes; there were no stars visible down here, so it must be something else that he was seeing. At the moment he did not question how such a structure had come to be here. The river itself flowed from somewhere beyond Allie's vision to a distant body of water that might have been an inland sea.

All around the slab of granite they had ridden were growing what could only be described as plants. Conifers above them, deciduous below, all with blue leaves. Short thin reeds that might have been related to cattails stood in random clusters. Bare rock showed through the groundcover, a weblike growth that might have been just one plant, spreading far and wide. The rock, in this area at least, was basaltic. To Allie, that meant they must have tumbled closer to the Mohorovičić discontinuity. It was not what he had expected to find. He doubted Andrija Mohorovičić would have expected it, either.

In the aftermath of the avalanche and the long slide, when dust and detritus and debris had finally settled into their new places, there began the most unexpected feature: sounds. A chirp here, a squawk there, a buzzing, and the thumps of heavier feet moving somewhere in the surrounding forest.

"Better open your eyes," Allie said in a low voice.

"Already open. *Groot god in die hemel!*"

Allie, who understood only the second word, nodded at her

inflection.

Mayane looked up. "I thought I saw," she began, and suddenly pointed. "There! That's our lift!"

"What remains of it." Dismay made his voice creak. "And there's part of the door. I think the entire mineshaft system, horizontal and vertical, has collapsed and become blocked."

"So we cannot go back up," she said, desolated. "And even if we could, we can't dig our way to the surface. And no one will be coming for us, thinking we are dead."

"Yeah."

"This is all your fault."

"I know. I'm sorry."

A loud sigh escaped her. "No, *I'm* sorry," she said quickly. "I did not mean to say that."

"Just exercising the words, were you?" But his grin forgave her.

She got to her feet and shook the dust from her hair. "But what are we going to do? We have no clothes other than what we're wearing. We have no food." She dug out her Palmetto and tokked it, examining the result. "We can't get a signal down here, and even if we could make contact, who would come for us?"

"Well, there's no point in going up," he said. "We can stay here, or we can go down and see what's there. I vote down."

"I vote we don't walk in front of this sled of granite," she said. "Just in case."

He peered over the side of the slab. "It's a drop of about ten, twelve feet," he told her. After letting the coil of rope fall, he shrugged out of the backpack. Loosening enough rope to reach the ground, he looped the rest around a rough edge and tugged on it to test its security.

Mayane understood immediately. "I could hold the rope," she offered.

"It's not necessary. Just free it after I'm down and toss it over."

That lost her. "But...what about me?"

"I'll catch you. I'll steady you. You'll be all right."

Carefully he went over the side and lowered himself to the ground. At his signal, she pitched the backpack down to him, followed by the flashlight, and finally by the rope.

"It looks so far down," she said not hiding her concern.

"Sit down on the edge," he told her. "That will take a little distance off your jump." He held his arms out for her. "Whenever you're ready, Tha...*Mej* Mayane."

"If you catch me, you can call me Thadie."

"That'll save syllables. Jump!"

He caught her just before her feet hit the ground, and staggered back a few steps, retaining his balance. To Allie's mild astonishment, they remained upright. At her frosty, "You can let go now," he released her, and retrieved his backpack and flashlight.

All around them grew knee-high variegated blades of blue with dull yellow edging, a possible analog of prairie grass. He noticed about half the blades came to points, while the other half had flat ends, as if the points had been bitten off. He looked for signs of whatever might have eaten them, including droppings, but found nothing to confirm grazing animals were in the area. Mayane noticed them as well and kept a sharp lookout as they headed down the slope toward the forest.

Mayane wore wonder on her face like a badge of honor; Allie supposed his own expression reflected hers. They walked slowly, a caution against surprising a denizen of the grass. He wished he had a walking stick, to sweep across the ground in front of him and bestir whatever lurked there. To that end, he used his knife to cut a brace of saplings, six feet long and two inches in diameter at the base and gave one to Mayane.

She examined the stick. "This isn't bark," she announced. "It feels almost like leather. It's flexible."

"That's the stick itself," he scoffed.

"No, look." She pinched two fingers against the outer covering of the stick, so that it bunched up between them like a thin layer of body fat.

They walked on. "I guess I shouldn't be surprised to find life down here," he said. "This is, after all, where life originated on Earth: deep underground."

"You cannot be serious."

He stepped over a couple narrow, shallow washes. "There was an article about it back in June of twenty twenty-two," he recalled. "It seems the primordial Earth of four billion years ago was inhospitable on the surface. Volcanoes, earthquakes, no water, no oxygen, asteroids still hitting the planet. There was no way life could form on the surface. Yet it did develop, all those years ago. We find traces of organic matter in rocks that are four billion years old. We find microbes, even today, alive at a depth of almost three kilometers." He glanced up at the light. "This is Pellucidar. Burroughs was right."

Her brow knotted. "But...you said no oxygen. Yet we are breathing here."

"The original life underground was anaerobic," he pointed out. "Oxygen was poisonous to it. Some of these plant analogs we're seeing may still be a little anaerobic, especially in internal processes where oxygen does not reach. But these plantalogs overall grow densely enough to oxygenize the air. And our atmosphere could have leaked down here. Deep mines, crevasses in the crust. Subduction could have opened up fissures. So: as above, so below."

Mayane shook her head. "No. It wouldn't have evolved the same way as on the surface. This stick is proof of that."

"Yeah." He looked around. "I wonder what else evolved down here."

"It would be very different."

"Something has been eating this grass," he pointed out. "That means herbivores. Carnivores eat herbivores; otherwise, we'd all be up to our necks in herbivores. Well, it's early days, yet."

"We need to find a safe place to sleep for the night," Mayane said.

Allie looked up again. "I don't think there is a night down here."

She gestured toward the tree line not far ahead. "Do we really want to go into that?"

"Water, first," he answered. "The river's on the other side of this forest." He drew a wrist across his forehead; he was sweating again—not so much from the temperature, which was moderate, but from the humidity and activity. A glance at Mayane told him she was experiencing the same discomfort. "We're losing water," he said, unnecessarily. "We have to find a source of it. Food can wait."

"You didn't bring any food?" she asked, amazed.

"Two boxes of granola bars," he said. "A few tins of smoked fish. Some bags of LRRPs. I hadn't planned to stay forever."

She paused to stare at him. "Some...what?"

"Long range reconnaissance patrol," he said. "LRRP. Rations for military patrols who don't often get back to base. It's mostly dehydrated grains; just add warm wat...*stop!*"

Thadie obeyed instantly, alarm in her dark eyes.

Allie prodded the end of his walking stick against a clump of grass growing next to a boulder of basalt, barely a step away from her feet. Something scurried from the grass to under the rock. He did not bend down and peer closer to see what it was. Gingerly, Thadie rounded the boulder, and they continued on toward the forest.

"I saw a little movement, and some dirt scatter," he explained. "Thanks for not saying, 'Huh?' and taking another step or two when I called for you to stop."

She would not look at him. "It's…difficult for me," she whispered, her voice just audible. "Any time I'm…there's a, a white man…"

Allie nodded, but without pressing the issue of race. "We don't know what dangers there are here," he told her, deliberately belaboring the obvious. "We have to protect each other; there's no one else here to do it. Believe me, if you see something and yell, 'Stop,' I'm a statue."

She almost laughed. "Deal. I'll even shoo the bloody pigeons away."

He glanced up. "I think we're about to get some rain."

"What's that?" she said, pointing ahead. "That looks like, like a, a trail of some kind."

"I think you're right."

Even as he spoke, lightning flashed above, followed by a long peal of thunder. Both came from behind them. Turning around, they saw the gathering mist had become a great bank of dark gray clouds hovering over the upper slope they had just descended. Already a pale gray sheet of rain was pummeling the slope behind them. Mindful of the washes he stepped over, and others he noticed, he turned a grim face to Thadie.

"We may have a problem," he said.

They increased their speed toward the forest. Allie could not say how much time they had to traverse five hundred yards. He might have run, but he doubted Thadie could keep up with him, and he refused to leave her behind and seek safety for himself. She kept to his pace, unwilling to leave him behind.

The downpour began to envelope them. A great sheet of rain deluged the upper slope. As Thadie glanced back, he said, "Don't look back. That just slows you down. We just keep going." His breath came raggedly now. "And Thadie," he gasped, "I know you're faster; I can tell. You go on."

"No!" She shoved him onward. "We go together."

"Damn it," he hissed, picking up his pace.

She stayed alongside him. At one point he stumbled, a misstep as his weight collapsed the bank of a dry wash, and she caught him, holding him upright until he regained his balance. But she released him as quickly as possible. In doing so, she glanced back and swore in a harsh language.

"We're not going to make it," she told him. He watched her keenly; she was not even breathing hard.

The backpack was slowing him down. The choice left to him was terrible: rid himself of it, and run faster, only to lose everything inside it; or keep it with him and drown in the onrushing waters. The waters gave him no time to decide. They struck with the force of a tsunami. He pitched forward into the surf, only to be pushed forward over rough terrain and rocks. He had lost sight of Thadie Mayane. Muddy water filled his mouth as he tried to call out to her. The side of his head struck a boulder, and his mind faded. He rolled sideways, once, twice. An uprooted tree fell over his shoulders. He dared not breathe, but he had to breathe. Crying out, he only managed to gargle. The light inside him grew dimmer, dimmer…

003: Up From the Microbes

Had Aldon McIntyre given the matter due consideration, he would have listed the first thing he wanted to greet his eyes when he awoke was the Zulu woman, Thadie Mayane. The very last thing he would have listed, well below a hot fudge sundae or even a fast-food restaurant, was another human being. With the man coming into focus, Allie sat up abruptly, and immediately fell back, his head swimming.

"Take it easy," the man said. He was paler than Allie, but roughly his equal in size. "You have had a tough go. You and your missus are lucky to be alive."

No, Allie thought, perfect English was at the bottom of that list.

A woman's scream cut through the humid air. Desperate to stand, Allie struggled to his knees, and once again fell back.

"It is all right," the man said. "She probably saw someone who hadn't changed. I promise you, nothing bad will happen to her in our moiety. Or to you."

A million questions formed. Allie's accusation scattered them like pigeons. "You took my clothes off."

"They are almost dry."

"And...and my backpack?"

"It is rather damp, but there is nothing that will not dry out." He made a desultory gesture. "It is just behind you, along with your equipment belt. I will say this: it is a good job the Oiskin didn't find you first." At Allie's confused look, he added, "Another moiety. Their territory abuts ours on the other side of the Fiumna...the river."

Allie finally looked around. "I'm in the forest," he said. "I don't understand."

"All in good time." He extended a forearm. "I am Gullaf. Your missus said you were Aldon."

Allie banged forearms with him. It seemed the thing to do. "Allie is fine," he said. Slightly embarrassed, he added, "She's not my 'missus.' We're..." He paused to consider. What in fact was Thadie Mayane to him? Having rescued one another now and then was hardly a relationship. "We're traveling together," he said. "Nothing more."

Gullaf looked dubious. "If you say so." He stood up and held out a hand for Allie to take. "Let us find out whether you can stand now."

Allie rose, trembled, and finally gained his feet, though his knees wobbled, and his head was still an Impressionist painting, not very lucid. He drew a few breaths that helped to steady him.

"Your missus…companion is right over here," Gullaf said, leading the way. Standing, he seemed a couple inches shorter than Allie, but about the same weight. His hair, like Allie's was dark brown. He was attired in loose brown pants and shirt, both of which appeared to be parchment. His feet were shod in bast.

"Were her clothes removed as well?" Allie asked.

"Yes." He paused in mid-step. "Is that a problem?"

"I…don't think I should see her naked," Allie said. He was trying not to imagine what Thadie would do to him if he saw her.

"Then I suspect the reverse is also true. Your clothes are hanging on that rack."

The "rack" turned out to be saplings trained to interweave among themselves. Their leaves were pale blue, shaped like tubes, and sparse. Quickly Allie drew his clothes back on, except for his boots, which he carried in his left hand.

They reached a tree network reminiscent of a banyan, though the oval, dark blue leaves were as soft as down. "Wait here, then," Gullaf said, and went on.

Steps had been added to various trunks of the network. Allie tested them, and managed to climb to the next level, an arbor where someone had slept before. He hoped he was not intruding as he stretched out on the network there. The fine branches yielded gently under his weight; he decided to sit up, to prevent himself from falling asleep there.

Even so, he dozed and was awakened by Thadie calling to him from below. Carefully he climbed down.

She was standing beside a taller black man dressed much the same as Gullaf. Evidently her clothes had not dried sufficiently, for she was wearing what he could only describe as a shift of parchment. It covered her from shoulders to mid-thigh. She seemed to be in good spirits, and even wore an unexpected smile for him as she drew up to him.

"It's amazing," she said. "There are black folk here, all of them are black."

That startled him. "What about Gullaf?"

She made a little gesture. "This *is* Gullaf."

Allie decided he could only conclude Gullaf was either a common name or a family name. "Was that you I heard scream?" he asked.

An embarrassed smile flickered across her face. "I could swear I saw a chimpanzee, or something very like one," she told him. "Otero said they meant me no harm." She looked him over. "Are you all right?"

"Physically, yes."

"I know what you mean." They made for the banyan where Allie had rested. "Why did you think that Gullaf was a white man?" she asked.

"Well, he...he was."

She shook her head. "Everyone I've seen here is black." She eyed him warily. "Why would you say...well, that's just typical, isn't it?" She came to a stop and turned away. "I might have known. You only see white folk."

"That's not fair—" But she had already begun walking away.

For a moment he debated whether to follow her. But her rigid spine said she was adamantine. He had no chance of explaining himself. Feeling wilted, he rested against a banyan trunk.

Not a minute later, a shrill whistle shattered the peaceful forest. Allie came bolt upright as Gullaf, now white, ran up to him. "It is the Oiskin," he said quickly. "We will be safe. But you cannot join us. Your best chance is to climb high into the network and keep silent and very still. Go, go!"

Allie did not budge. "What about Thadie?" he demanded.

"She is being seen to," Gullaf assured him, and dashed away.

Allie climbed, but reluctantly. Concern for Thadie threatened to overwhelm him. And what sort of danger did the Oiskins pose? What if this was a raid for mates? Such was not unheard of Above. Thadie...?

Yet Gullaf had said she was being seen to. What did that mean?

If this was a raid, how would Gullaf's moiety defend itself? Allie saw no preparations for defense. He began to feel that he had to do—

Movement below froze him. Allie peered hard through the foliage and the network. Incredible shapes resolved themselves in his view. His heart raced while he counted five of them. Simian impressions, at first, but he soon noticed they walked fully upright. Orange-brown hair, but not hirsute. Arms longer than human. Three were carrying wooden spears with fire-hardened tips. As they moved about, they seemed to be talking among themselves, chittering incomprehensibly. Gradually they disappeared from his view, but not before he realized they were reminiscent of Neandertals.

Suddenly a series of roars shook the forest. More than one predator was about. Now the chittering grew agitated, even panicked. Allie heard bodies crashing through the shrubs and understory. More roars followed, until two behemoths in black and gray fur charged past his tree network. Quadrupeds, and about the size of pickup trucks, they looked as if they might be herbivores. But there was no mistaking their carnivorous intent. One of the primitives turned and cast his spear, striking one of the quadrupeds in the shoulder. It scarcely seemed to notice the injury.

The roars and chittering gradually diminished to indeterminate sounds of the forest. It was over, Allie thought, but he dared not risk movement yet.

Still Allie did not move from his perch. Unable now to see them, he nevertheless continued to hear them. Desperation set in, out of concern for Thadie. Where was Gullaf, to tell him the danger had passed? He shifted position until he had a clearer view below. Nothing moved except a few leaves fluttering in a light breeze.

Allie heard, rather than saw, Gullaf. "You can come down now," he said.

Allie hastily complied, anxious to see Thadie again, to know she had not been harmed. Instead, he saw a black Gullaf and another man, also black.

"This is Otero," Gullaf said. "He has seen to your companion."

Allie's voice shook. "Where is she? And what were those things?"

Gullaf glanced back and winced. Rubbing his shoulder, he said, "She will be here presently. Are you all right?" After Allie's nod, he went on, "This happens often. The boundary between our two moieties has been fluid for some time now. Fortunately, our dietary needs are different. The Oiskin consume meat, which they hunt. We are more...your term would be agricul—ah, here she comes."

Allie resisted the impulse to run to her. Instead, he casually stepped forward and asked how she was.

She ignored him.

Gullaf turned to her but spoke to him. "She is quite all right, as you see." His head tilted to one side, as if he were thinking. "But I do not understand this relationship."

"There is no relationship," Thadie snapped. "He's white. He only sees white."

Gullaf nodded slowly, as if that explained everything. "Then this is my error, and Otero's, and that of others," he told her. "We thought our…respective coloration and appearance would make you more comfortable. But in presenting the two of you with two different colors, we have only made matters worse. Otero," he finished, in the tone of an instruction.

Both men began to alter themselves. Within seconds they reverted to bipeds covered with scales of various shades of green, like camouflage paint. There were other colors as well. Blue on the throats, pale lilac on the palms of the hands, each of which ended in three digits and an opposable thumb, all webbed to the first knuckle. Their heads were human, with yellow eyes and with black vertical slits for irises. The nose and lips jutted just a little. Allie was unable to see their teeth. The men's clothing had vanished, as if it had been a physical part of them and not merely an outer garment. There was no sign of any external reproductive organs.

To Allie, the transfer said color was irrelevant, and the contents within were all that mattered. This he understood directly; he wondered what Thadie saw.

"What," she gasped.

"The fuck," he finished for her.

004: Dinner and a Show

A campfire was started with the use of small sticks tipped with phosphorus. Gullaf and Otero and two others of their moiety, evidently female, sat around the fire, along with Allie and a pensive and contrite Thadie. Flickering flames cast their faces and bodies in light and shadow. One by one, other small fires erupted around them. With explanations in order—in demand, in fact—no one seemed eager to speak first. Allie had already begun to think in terms of the subterranean evolutionary process.

While each gathered thoughts, a round of food was deemed to be in order. A wooden bowl, evidently hand-carved, was brought in, and placed where the coals would warm it. It was filled with vegetable matter in the form of irregular blue and purple spheres, each roughly the size of a human thumb. In Allie's experience, any vegetable that turned blue was to be thrown out, and a fresh one purchased. Knowing he had to be courteous and try one, he reached out and was stopped by Otero.

Otero, grasping both of Allie's hands, held them out, while Beterr, one of the females, poured cool water over them from a clay pitcher. This accomplished, she dried his hands on a rough but absorbent sheet of parchment. He was then allowed to resume his seat. Thadie experienced the same cleansing; she sat across the fire from him. One by one in turn, the others had their hands cleansed, with Ssakileh pouring water over Beterr's hands and drying them.

"Now we may eat," Gullaf said, motioning for Allie to pick up the bowl.

Taking a warm blue ball from the bowl, Allie nibbled at it cautiously, while smiling at everyone. The taste vaguely suggested that of a barbecued Brussels sprout dipped in honey. After a few nibbles, he found it rather palatable, and nodded his approval at Thadie, watching him from across the fire, shadows playing on her skin.

The round completed—what Allie thought of as the first course —Gullaf eyed him speculatively, his scaled snout not a foot away from Allie's face. "Would you feel more comfortable if we appeared as you do?" he asked.

To Allie, it felt gauche to suggest someone alter his appearance to one that was regarded as more convenient or pleasing. Before he could respond, however, Thadie spoke.

"I-I don't understand how you can…how you are able to do that," she said. She barked a dry laugh. "Or how you can speak English, or how…how you can even be here."

"It is simple to explain," Ssakileh said beside her. She was the only one with a purple snout. She spread her hands—each with three fingers and an opposable thumb, all webbed—in a plea for understanding. "We are how we are."

The response clearly failed to satisfy Thadie, who raised a black eyebrow at Allie. He felt a moment of relief that she had turned to him for answers, even if they were answers he might not have, and despite her spasms of animosity toward him.

Given a moment of thought, he said, "It's protective mimicry. It's a defense mechanism. For example, there is a giant cockroach in Costa Rica. It grows to about four inches. In coloration and shape, it looks exactly like a dead leaf, inedible to a predator. There are chameleons, which I'm sure you know about. There is a fish with a black dot on its tail to make a predator think that marks the head end. These folks have simply evolved an advanced form of that defense mechanism." He paused, and added lightly, seeing her expression, "There will be a quiz."

She did not laugh. "And the English?"

"I have no idea. Telepathy, perhaps? Or maybe we just hear English?"

Thadie looked doubtful. "But then he would know to speak Afrikaans or Zulu to me."

"*Ek praat Afrikaans, as jy wil*," Gullaf told her.

"I-I really don't understand how…" she said.

He reverted to English. "We have a receiver that acquires transmissions from Above," he told her.

"I thought I saw a dish antenna by the river as we came down the slope," Allie said. "I thought it was a mirage."

"It's no mirage," Gullaf assured him. "Television and radio, mostly. Over the years, as you regard them, we have learned the languages in which those transmissions are sent. We have also received imagery—television, and transmissions from your satellites—and what you call 'streaming,' although we have yet to unlock its coding.

Oh, yes, we are very much aware of Above." His tone dropped an octave. "And we are very much afraid of it."

"But why?" Allie asked.

"In your terms, it is because of the way Life is hard-wired," Ssakileh answered.

Otero made his excuses and went to fetch another wooden bowl. This one proved to contain dark green berries the size of the tip of Allie's little finger. He tried one, and found it gave off pungent fumes when crushed between the teeth. He spat his out and coughed.

"Do not chew them," Beterr said. "Swallow them whole, with water, if that will help."

Allie succeeded on the next attempt, although he was concerned for what the fumes might do later in his digestive tract.

"These are called *yagoah*," Gullaf said, in answer to an unspoken question.

"How do you know what to…?" Thadie began, then stopped. She stared hard at Gullaf. "You have fed people from Above before this." It was not quite an accusation.

Gullaf admitted as much. "There have been several who have come and remained down here. Not all of them with us, of course. You are the third and fourth to stay with us."

Allie looked around. "Where are the other two?" he asked.

"Abner Perry passed on about eighty of your years ago…"

"Wait," Allie said. "You said 'your years.' And earlier you referred to 'years, as you regard them.' But our years are measured by an orbital journey around the sun. How can you possibly know how to measure that?"

Ssakileh nodded. "Do not be misled by our simple campfires. We Alassal and other moieties have developed our…sciences. One example is the dish antenna we use to capture transmissions from Above. The matter of time was resolved in the short term by the waves of our seas, and in the long term by our measurements of the mass of a standard object." She smiled benignly. "We have in fact no use whatsoever for your leap year."

The tip of Thadie's tongue moistened her lips in anticipation of enlightenment. "You…you're talking about tides."

Ssakileh hissed approval. "And in the long term?" she asked, testing.

"I-I have no idea," Thadie said, gazing across the fire at Allie for help.

Allie shook his head. "I don't know…but to measure a year accurately, you would have to at least be aware of the sun's existence…"

"Or aware of the existence of such a mass," Gullaf hinted. "We interpolated its existence from our measurements."

Allie sat back. "Oh, I see."

"What?" Thadie said. "Tell me."

"Well…you would have to have very sensitive instruments," he began.

"We do. Go on."

"You would have noticed the changes in gravitational pull as the moon moved in its orbit around the Earth. This would have given you the concept of a month."

Gullaf hissed his approval. "Aces, as you say. Do continue."

Allie spoke more quickly, now that understanding had crept in. "But with instruments that are sensitive enough, you would have noticed the pull varied in another way, once you subtracted the effects of the moon from your results."

"Almost there," Otero said.

"That pull varies with the distance from the sun. I don't recall the exact distances, but in the Earth's orbit around the sun, Earth is ninety-one million miles at its closest, and ninety-four million at its farthest. You would not be able to measure that, of course—"

"Have another *yagoah*," Beterr said.

"Thank you." Allie remembered not to chew it. "But you would be able to measure the pull of the sun's gravity. You must have noticed that periodically the mass of some object here…Below?"

"Below, yes," Beterr said.

"That periodically the mass was identical to that which it had been earlier. The period of time—and you could measure this period by any one of several simple means—between two identical measurements, you would define as a year." He finished lightly. "Or whatever your word for 'year' is."

"In fact, Allie," Ssakileh said, "we call it a year. But well done! Very well done!"

Approval warmed Allie's face.

"You said Allie and I were third and fourth," Thadie reminded them. "Who was second?"

"That was a man named David," Otero replied. "He stayed with us for several high tides, and then…vanished. No one knows what happened to him."

"Klonx was most distraught," Beterr added. "She was…quite taken with him."

Allie frowned hard. "You mean…you mean she and…and…"

"Yes, of course," Ssakileh said. "When you love someone, you love someone. It is that simple. And it is something you humans still have to learn." She sighed, a breath of air that flared her nostrils. "You have too many rules."

"Ssakileh," Otero said softly.

She inclined her head. "Yes, of course. You are right. I forget myself."

Beterr brought forward a third bowl, this one deeper than the other two. She offered it to Thadie first. She peered into the bowl, and a question formed on her face.

"You would call this smoked fish," Beterr said.

A wry expression crossed Allie's face when the bowl reached him. He was unaccustomed to eating sardines with his fingers. *When in Rome*, he thought. That depressed him, for he realized he probably would never see Rome again.

"Are you all right?" Ssakileh asked, while he chewed.

He dismissed the question, "Just a passing thought."

"But it has saddened you," she pressed.

Before he could respond, she rose and brought another bowl to the group, serving Allie first. The fourth course proved to be the last, a dessert consisting of bits of dried fruit, none of which he recognized. He selected three at random and thanked her.

A silence ensued that was both comfortable and uneasy. It had a what-now flavor to it. With the overhanging trees blotting some of the light from the vaulted ceiling, Allie had the feeling the time for sleep was almost upon them. But there was no "day" or "night" Below. There was only time, and its unfamiliar measurements. He looked to Gullaf for guidance.

"You are correct," Gullaf said, reading his expression. "This is when we rest and sleep. We sleep in the *sevvyls*…the trees. The temperature will remain as it is; you need not concern yourself for warmth. I suggest the spot where you hid from the Oiskin, for no one has claimed it. Do you know the way?"

Allie nodded. "I think so." He got up to leave, but once again Otero stopped him, and took Allie's hands in his. A moment later, Ssakileh poured water over them, thus initiating the closing process to the meal…

~ * ~

Allie decided he was already becoming accustomed to the forest and its ways. As he climbed up onto the arbor, the soft and yielding leaves cushioned him. It was only a matter of a moment or two before he felt himself dozing off. The meal with the Alassals had not sated him but had been sufficient for him to take some time digesting it.

A light tremor in the tree brought Allie fully alert. Had Gullaf been mistaken; had someone claimed this spot, after all? Eyes narrowed; he looked down through the foliage, but saw no one ascending. Perhaps it was the wind, or even his imagination. He was just about to settle back onto the bed of leaves when a deep purple nose and mouth poked through the foliage on the other side of him.

Slowly, as if to avoid alarming him, Ssakileh came into view, and sat beside him.

"Um," Allie muttered, all other words had fled.

"You were sad," she said.

He collected himself and his voice. "Yeah, I guess I was," he conceded. "Ssakileh…what are you doing here?"

"Do you not know? Can you not guess?"

Flustered, he lost his voice again.

"Your companion sleeps alone," Ssakileh said. "I must conclude she is not your *ssenya*, and you are free to choose…or to choose not. If you wish it, I would spend this sleep with you."

"Sleep," he repeated heavily.

She hissed approval. "Perhaps not so much sleep."

"Ssakileh, I-I…"

When he did not finish, she spoke softly. "That is not a no."

"Even if…I mean…how can we?"

Her hands fluttered. "You have external genitalia," she said. "I have internal. It is a good fit. I will guide you."

"B-but…"

"Do not be concerned for offspring," Ssakileh said. "We would need a genetic splice if the egg is to be fertilized."

"That…that wasn't…" He paused, uncertain as to what it was not.

"Then…is it that you wish me to change?"

"Change?"

"To a form more…appealing."

"Um…um, no."

The expression that formed on her face was unreadable. "If you tell me you do not want to share this space with me, Allie, I will leave."

What he wanted was a tree trunk to bang his head against—several times. Instead, he closed his eyes, intending to test whether he was already asleep. When he opened them again, she was still there, waiting patiently for his acceptance or his rejection. Evidently, he was awake.

His thought was that his high school sex education instructor would never believe this.

Taking a deep breath, he patted the leaves beside him.

005: When in Rome

Allie woke and sensed it should have been morning. Disoriented at first, he soon recalled his circumstances. The leaves beside him were still flattened, but Ssakileh had already departed, an empty space inside him. In his bed life he had in the past taken a moment's pleasure in simply waking up to someone. But this might not be the Alassal way; it was not something he and Ssakileh had discussed. There had not, in fact, been much discussion at all.

From his vantage point, Allie now saw the Alassal encampment was located on a broad, flat-top hill, and well above the flood line. Toward the river he saw three different structures of cut stone, each roughly the size of a two-story house, with gabled roofs and with windows at least on the upper levels, which was all the forest would allow him to see from this vantage. In one window, a light was on, but he saw no movement within; a good hundred yards away, details were scarce.

After two yawns and a languid stretch, Allie climbed down and began to look for his backpack. He found it near the site of the campfire, under a large bush with red-violet flowers. He also encountered Gullaf, who was once again white.

"Very disconcerting," Allie said, by way of greeting. "May I ask?"

"Of course, Allie."

"Those…creatures that chased the Oiskins away, they were you?"

"Myself and Ssakileh, yes." He rubbed his shoulder again. "Unfortunately, changing shape does not lend itself to invulnerability." He glanced toward a small clearing. "Ssakileh is over there," he said. His eyes flicked up. "And your traveling companion is still asleep."

"Gullaf…what happens now?"

"What do you mean?"

Allie struggled for words. "Well, I…we can't go back…can we?"

"I am sorry."

"Then…what do I do here? What does Thadie do?"

For a moment, Gullaf hesitated. With a little sweep of his hand, he bade Allie follow him. Five minutes later, they reached the bank of a creek that was still somewhat flooded from the cloudburst and sat down on the lush grass there. Dangling their legs over the edge of the bank left their soles a good three feet above the burbling waters.

After a few quiet moments of reflection, Gullaf spoke. "The question is, what *can* the two of you do? Thadie is a mining supervisor, and we do have mines here. Perhaps your own work is related?"

"I test water quality Above," Allie told him. "My education was in organic chemistry, and my avocation is geology." He flashed a sheepish grin. "That's probably not a lot of help."

"We monitor our sources of water. Most moieties do this. You might be interested in the procedures. Geology might enable you to study terrain and identify new areas of mining interest."

"I suppose I could teach as well," Allie said.

"First, you would have to learn and to unlearn. Allie…we are aware of society Above. What you have experienced there is almost nothing like society Below." His voice dropped to a whisper. "We were appalled by much of what we learned of Above after we began to analyze their transmissions."

"I can imagine," Allie said grimly.

"While we are aware of matters Above," Gullaf continued in the same tone, "we do not allow them to taint us or our thinking. In fact, we have therapeutic occupations that deal with those who are not strong enough to prevent some portion of the evils Above from affecting them. You may want to avail yourself of such a therapist."

The general nature of the briefing by Gullaf left Allie with too many questions. "What sort of 'matters Above' are you talking about?" he asked.

Gullaf muttered a few words to himself, incomprehensible to Allie, as if he were attempting to isolate a cogent paradigm. "You place great stock in the concept of freedom and rights, Allie," he finally said. "Yet it often appears to us, from what we can glean from broadcasts, your freedom is inversely proportional to the number of rights you have. For example, you have the right to be offended by the remarks of another, to the extreme extent of diminishing that individual's freedom of speech in order to defend your right not to be offended." His eyes met Allie's. "Is this not so?"

"Well…well, yes, I suppose, but…"

"That is not possible here," Gullaf said. "If you do not wish to listen to what someone has to say, you walk away."

Right away Allie had an objection. "What if the speaker follows you, and continues to talk at you? What, then?"

Gullaf shook his head. "But that would be unthinkable here," he said. "It is not the way we are. Even the Oiskin, as primitive as they are, would never compel anyone to listen. No, Allie, you listen as you choose to.

"Furthermore, your sexual relationships are based on possession. To be fixed into such a relationship, you must obtain the sanction of your government and in many cases, your church. You have an abundance of sexually possessive terms in your daily vocabulary. 'Going steady,' 'main squeeze,' to name just two. 'Heartbreak' occurs when a sexual relationship is ended, thus confirming the possessive nature of that relationship. Your so-called 'soap-operas' are replete with illicit sexual relationships, illicit because of the guilt that attaches to someone who draws another out of their relationship. Is not 'home-wrecker' one of your terms? What about 'cuckold?' Does not the term 'steal you away' imply possession? Do you not use possessive pronouns in your language when you speak of husbands, wives, lovers?"

Allie, thinking of Ssakileh, asked, "And how is it different here Below?"

"You are thinking of Ssakileh—"

"Are you telepathic?" Allie asked abruptly.

"Yes." While Allie gaped at him, he asked, "May I continue?"

Allie, with a hundred questions dammed up inside him, could only nod.

"Yes," Gullaf said again, "but we are not intrusive with it. I was not reading your mind. I was analyzing your tells…your expressions, the shifts of your eyes, the twitch of your nose, the way your shoulders tensed when I mentioned her name."

Gullaf paused for a moment, as if nerving himself to pursue the topic. "You want to ask how it is here, Allie. Very well. Ssakileh is… fond of you. But she would be equally fond of you if you had contiguous relationships with a hundred others and she had to wait her turn. Your other relationships would not cause her to feel jealousy or take offense. She might wait until you asked her to visit you again; or she might visit you, as she did during our sleep time, to find out whether you wanted her with you for that time. For that matter, if I wanted to visit you, or you me, I would simply show up and ask."

Allie shifted uncomfortably. "This is all…awkward."

"Because of the social and emotional suitcase you brought with you."

"Baggage," Allie said automatically. "Emotional baggage."

"Thank you. Yes, baggage." He smiled. "I see you have another question."

"I-I…yes, I…is exclusivity possible in a relationship?"

Gullaf nodded. "Certainly, if all parties consent to—"

"Both parties, you mean."

"I did not say 'both,' Allie."

The realization momentarily overwhelmed Allie. He leaned back, braced on stiff arms, and tried to clear his head. Although familiar with the idea of polyamory, he had not encountered so blithe and open a practice. "I think," he began, and stopped to collect fragments of thought. "I think the concept of 'all' would negate individual possession in relationships. It would require group possession, however, but in a sense of belonging, not of ownership. Everyone in the group would have to…to…"

"Consent," Gullaf supplied. He leaned back as well. "I believe you understand now, Allie. From the stories handed down, that is far more than Abner Perry ever understood, in all his time here."

Allie glanced at Gullaf, then looked at him sharply. "You're mentoring me," he said. It was not quite an accusation.

"As Ssakileh and Mollow are at this moment mentoring Thadie," Gullaf said. "It is our way of inviting you into our moiety. You do not have to accept, of course." A tiny frown of curiosity bunched over his brow. "Ssakileh asked you this when she came to you, about shifting to an appearance that might please you more."

Allie gasped. "You know about that? She told you that?"

"Yes, of course."

"I did not realize I would be the subject of a report," he groused. Almost immediately a flash of insight brightened him. "Oh, wait. In a society such as yours, there could be nothing private about sexual relations." He sighed. "This is going to take some getting used to. Just when I understand something, another mystery arises."

Gullaf brushed the comment aside. "Yet you permitted Ssakileh to remain in her primary form during her visit. Would you tell me why you did that?"

"I-I don't know why," he said, fumbling his way. "It-it just felt

…I don't know."

"It is okay—"

"Why should anyone have to change what they look like for the sake of someone else's comfort?" Allie blurted. "You are who you are."

Gullaf smiled tolerantly. "Yet cosmetics is a major human industry," he pointed out. "You adjust your appearance to one more pleasing, insofar as you are capable."

"But I am among you," Allie argued. "You are not among me." He had a pained look. "I'm not sure that's the best way to say that."

For the first time during the course of this encounter, Gullaf laid a reassuring hand on Allie's shoulder. "I understand," he said. "More to the point, you understand, and even more so, you accept." He looked away. "It may be that such understanding will be difficult for Thadie. She has some…you would call them issues…"

"No, I wouldn't. I would refer to them as problems. Are you talking about her attitude toward me? Or the difference in our attitudes toward each other?"

"She regards you as a white man," Gullaf replied. "You think of her as a woman who is black. Do you see the difference? Just as—if I may be permitted to say this—you think of Ssakileh as a person, whole and self-contained."

"I had not put it into words."

A brief and languid silence followed, broken by Gullaf. "Are you hungry?" he asked.

"Yes." He amended that to, "A little."

"Come with me."

~ * ~

Allie found himself at the campfire site, although this time no kindling had been ignited. Already others had gathered around it— Ssakileh and Beterr bracketing a somewhat disconsolate Thadie Mayane, and another female Alassal who was likely Mollow. All the Alassals except Gullaf were in their primary form. Even as Allie sat down, Otero joined them. This time it was Mollow who managed the hand-washing ceremony before food was passed around.

Very much aware Thadie would not meet his gaze, Allie soon abandoned the attempt to greet her. Perhaps she already knew of his liaison with Ssakileh; that would explain at least a part of her frosty attitude. If in poor spirits, she appeared to be in good health and was still wearing the pale yellow gown of parchment she had been given while her clothes dried. Her loose black hair had received the attention of a brush, and now glistened in the light that made it through the overhanging foliage. Allie found it interesting that in the afterglow of Ssakileh and the talk with Gullaf, he was looking at Thadie as a woman. But that was as far as the thought went. Whatever she had discussed with the Alassal females had only made her more intractable toward him.

The first bowl that was passed around, beginning with Thadie, contained a pale blue fruit the size and shape of a mahjool date, resembling it even to the pit inside. Allie took two and found them soft and sweet. Following the examples of the Alassals, he spat the pits onto the ground to one side.

Waiting for the next bowl to arrive, Allie glanced around the cold firepit. Now that he was more familiar with the Alassals, he noted no two snouts were alike, in that they were colored in a camouflage pattern and could be identified by the colors themselves. Where Ssakileh's was deep purple, that of Otero was orange and gray, Beterr was two different shades of green, and Mollow was a glossy medium brown. As there were a full two scores of Alassals, he wondered whether he should jot down some notes.

Soft-shelled nuts came next. They tasted vaguely of smoked garlic. He found them palatable and popular; the bowl was empty before it had completed the circumnavigation of the firepit and had to be refilled. Movement beside him caught his eye, and he glanced in that direction to find Gullaf had also transformed back to primary. Once again he looked across the firepit at Thadie, but she was speaking with Mollow and did not notice him. Or she was still ignoring him.

After the fifth and last bowl had gone around, the hand-washing ceremony was repeated, this time by Thadie. When she reached Allie, she went about her duty in a perfunctory manner, but for just a moment their eyes locked, and he flashed a winsome smile at her. The smile was not reciprocated, but he felt a decrease in the tension that oozed from her.

Baby steps, he thought.

006: Walkabout

After Thadie had completed her round, he whispered to Gullaf. "Is it all right if I wander around a little? Is there any place I should avoid?"

"You've heard our alarm system," Gullaf said. "If it sounds, take shelter as high as you can. One of us will come for you when it is clear."

Allie rose, and moved away, wondering who, if anyone, would follow him. He wove his way around saplings and shrubs, and crossed small open areas covered with flowering understory—small whites and bright oranges, mostly. He hated to step on the flowers, but there was no other way across.

On the other side of the last open area, the *sevvyls*—as the tree analogs were called—were sparse, and he thought he heard water flowing. Ahead, the ground sloped gently upward—an embankment. At his next step, he crushed a dry twig, or so he thought. But the sound had come from behind him. Forsaking expectations, he turned around.

Mollow of the glossy brown snout followed him. Seeing she was discovered, she hastened to explain. "It was thought you might need a guide. If you wish to cross the river, there is a bridge in that direction." She punctuated this with a little gesture to his left.

Allie found he was glad of the company, even if he had not been introduced.

They headed in the direction she indicated, and soon found themselves at a spot on the bank where the waterflow, bending away from the Alassal encampment, had undercut the ground and cause a few trees to topple into the water. Eddies swirled against the trunks and branches. Mollow, her attention fixed on the water, strolled out to what had been the upper branches of one of the trees. She leaned forward, peering into the water, four webbed digits on each hand spread in anticipation.

Allie, who had caught grunion on the coast of California, recognized what she was about. He tried to imagine what sort of life inhabited the rivers and waterways in what he had already come to think of as the Moho—not the discontinuity, but the land itself. Fish, aquatic reptiles, amphibians? Evolution would have taken different turns here in the Moho.

Mollow dove her head and upper body into the water, splashed briefly, and at last emerged with a long thin wriggler in her grasp. Above, it might have been an eel, but as she brought it toward Allie, he could see this eel had scales—something that true eels lacked. As she approached, she held the eel encircled by the fingers and thumb of both hands and gave the eel a wrench. It stopped wriggling immediately.

To Allie's utter astonishment, Mollow then opened a pouch on her upper abdomen and thrust the dead eel into it. "For food later," she explained. "I will set up a fire for us, and grill this…what is it, Allie? What is wrong?"

He averted his eyes from the pouch. "Nothing. Nothing's wrong. I just didn't know you had a…a…"

"Pouch. Yes, all females do, except Thadie." She paused while she used the edges of her hands to press water from her upper body. "Those who have offspring carry them in the pouches. This frees their hands for other work."

They resumed their journey toward the bridge, which was still not yet in sight. "How do you, um, nurse the young?" he asked.

Mollow's nostrils flared. "Nurse?"

"Feed?" he tried.

"Oh. With a utensil, of course." Realization dawned on her. "Oh! *That* is what those things are on Thadie's chest. Like the Lannar females have. Oh, now I understand." The scales over her eyes bunched. "But she seemed so reluctant to remove her shirt…"

"That," Allie said, "will require a lot of explanation."

"If I understand your question correctly, our 'young,' as you call them, eat the same food we do."

Rounding a hillock on the bank of the river, they drew within sight of the bridge. Constructed of ropes of a fiber Allie was unable to identify, the bridge swayed several feet above the water, held in place by its moorings—on the near side, a great thick tree, and on the far side, the stump of a tree that had been cut down. Here the river was, by Allie's estimate, only twenty feet wide or thereabouts. All in all, the bridge looked safe.

Well, it would have to be safe, he thought. *The Alassals use it.*

"Isn't that Oiskin territory?" he asked, pointing across the river.

"I promise you, Allie, you will be safe from them."

The bridge swayed even more as he followed Mollow across it. Reaching the other side, they jumped down onto the grassy bank. Allie lost his footing, and rolled a couple of times, ending up in the shade of a group of shrubs with yellow flowers edged in purple. As he sat up, she dropped down beside him. His nostrils drank in the aroma of the flowers and the slightly pungent tang of Mollow, and for a moment he wondered whether their placement here together had been contrived. Surely Ssakileh had related her tale of their intimacies. But Mollow sat still, gazing out over the river, her respiration slow and shallow.

"You wished to walk around," Mollow said softly. "What do you want to see?"

Allie shook his head. "I don't know. This is all new to me. I think I had better understand the land."

"And the rules," she added.

"Yes, of course." Then, alarmed: "Wait! Am I breaking a rule?"

She looked down at the lush blue grass between them. "When a male and a female go off together," she told him, "it is usually understood they will engage in what you call intimacies."

"Mollow…"

"It is not a very stiff rule," she added quickly, defensively.

"Rigid," he amended.

"Yes…rigid. A good word."

Allie had the grace to blush. He got to his feet and held out his hand to her. "Shall we?"

She demurred. "This is a comfortable place."

"I meant…" He made a wry face. "I meant, shall we continue our walk?"

Her face showed no trace of disappointment as she accepted the hand he offered. "If that is what you wish."

On the far side of the river, the forest became denser as they walked along the bank. The near side, mostly rolling to rugged grassland at first, became clotted with flowering shrubs, with more *sevyls*, or trees, beyond them. Here the floral aroma was stronger, and Allie's nose began to run. With no handkerchief in his pockets, he was forced to wipe his nose on his shirt.

"Allergies," he explained, embarrassed.

"What are those?" Mollow asked.

"A negative physiological reaction to, um, stimuli."

"Still I do not understand."

"Pollen makes me sneeze."

Mollow nodded. "Ah. That, I understand."

The temperature felt as if it had dropped a little. Allie looked up. Gray clouds had formed, reminiscent of cumulus. Their movement was almost imperceptible but was in their direction. "Are we in danger from flooding?" he asked her.

"I think it will be very wet, but no more than that," she replied. "Ahead there is a bend in the river, with an undercut above the water level. We may take refuge there."

"Is it safe?" Allie asked.

She quickened her pace, and he stayed with her. "I have waited there before, from the lightning."

That worried him. "Lightning?"

The clouds above spoke their piece.

"And thunder," she said, increasing her pace yet again.

They were within a dozen paces of the river bend when the first raindrops pelted them. Mollow led him down the embankment, on a path that had been used before, to a stretch of sand and pea-sized gravel. The sand on a raised bed above the current bore marks of many footprints; this was a frequented place of refuge. Ahead and to the right was a great overhang where the once-higher river had cut away the rock and exposed many tree roots. Ducking down, and taking his hand, Mollow led him well under the rock shelf and out of the rain.

Others had made their mark in the rock. Despite the darkness of the storm, Allie was able to make out various shapes etched into the granite and then colored with something like umber or sienna. The etchings were reminiscent of the wall paintings at Lascaux, although the representations were different.

He touched a finger to one of the scratched lines. "Who did this?" he asked Mollow. "Do you know?"

She spoke uncertainly. "It may have been one of the Degg moieties." As this response added to his frown, she explained, "They live on both sides of the river. There are two moieties, the Sevvyl Degg on the far side, and the Ravneen Degg on this side."

He continued to examine the etchings, but he was unable to

discern any specific features of the bipeds. "What do they look like?" he asked.

She had to think about that. "If you and I were mated and able to reproduce, the result might be a Degg," she said slowly. "Like me, but paler, and tan. I have not seen one up close. They are secretive, and territor...hush! Listen!"

The rain drowned out most of the sounds, but Allie thought he heard running footsteps, definitely bipedal. Suddenly into view came an Oiskin male, naked and orange-haired, and drenched. He skidded to a stop in the wet sand as he spotted Allie and Mollow. Warily he eyed them and glanced over his shoulder as if debating whether to abandon the shelter and flee. A flash of lightning nearby and a bang of thunder decided him. Cautiously he approached, then dashed forth as he came to understand the occupants of the shelter meant him no immediate harm. Even as he reached the overhang, both Allie and Mollow hustled him into the shelter. There they sat on the dry sand, two facing one across a distance measured both in space and in evolution.

Allie patted himself on the chest and spoke his name. The new arrival regarded him with curiosity and fear in his deep-set brown eyes.

"He will not understand your English," Mollow whispered.

"But why not? You do. It's your language."

She shook her head. "It is not our language. We only speak it in order to communicate with you and Thadie. But it does not matter. I speak only some of his words."

"He looks like one of those who were chased away from your encampment," he said. He started to add, "Yesterday," but time was not measured in that manner here.

The man gestured violently and yelled at them. Clearly, he was upset about something. Allie wished he knew what it was.

"He is suspicious," Mollow said. "We are supposed to speak in his language."

"How do you know...are you reading his mind?"

"Yes, of course. He is very primitive, and easy to read. His thoughts are simple, and motivated by fear, greed, and hunger. He would try to take our food, if we had any."

"Can you...project thoughts into him?"

"I can try. His needs are rudimentary. Hush, please."

For a few moments the man grew even more agitated. Soon, however, he began to settle down and calm himself. He edged away from them and reseated himself to gaze out at the rain. He picked at the hair on his arm, as if to catch small insects.

"I have calmed him," Mollow said. "But I do not know how long it will hold." She peered out and up at the rain. "It is going to last for a while."

"You're shivering," he said. "Are you cold?"

"A little."

"Sit closer to me."

When she leaned against him for warmth, he slipped an arm around her. Her body seemed to be the same temperature as the surrounding air. He wondered whether she was cold-blooded, like a reptile. But the question applied to him as well, for he, too, was chilled.

It was the scales, he decided, that made him question her temperature. Otherwise, her face and body were human, if one discounted the slightly prognathous mouth and jaw. A sigh failed to ease him. He knew he was idealizing her, and it was totally unnecessary.

"I have to learn the rules," he muttered. He felt her nod against his shoulder. "Are you reading me?" he asked.

She pulled her head back to look at him. "I am sorry."

"Mollow, why did you come with me on this walk?"

"To protect you," she answered, as if that should have been obvious.

"Is that…the only reason?"

She hissed a laugh. "No, of course not."

He thought about that for a moment. "I wish it would stop raining."

"Why?"

"So he would leave," he said, and she laughed again.

"He will not watch us," she assured him.

~ * ~

Allie had no idea how much time had passed. The rain seemed to be lighter, and the Oiskin was gone. Best of all, he was now warmer. He did not jostle Mollow as he gently drew his clothes back on, but she came awake with a start as he began to lace and tie his boots. She waited until he had finished, then tagged his arm. "Come with me," she said.

They went to the edge of the river and knelt down on the sand. While Allie held out his hands, she gathered up water in hers and poured it over them. When she held out her hands expectantly, he performed the same ritual for her.

Mollow sat back. "Now we may eat," she announced, and rummaged around in her pouch for edibles.

The meal consisted of bits of fruit Allie found palatable, and some nuts that had been roasted. It was not a full meal, but it would sustain them for a while.

"We will find some more fruit further along the river," she assured him. "Ready?"

But as they turned to face the riverbank, they were confronted by five Oiskins, all armed with spears with fire-hardened tips.

"Now what do we do?" Allie asked.

"I do not know," she whispered. "On the few occasions when they intrude into our territory, we have already become something else to frighten them away. I am not certain they have ever seen one of us as we truly appear."

"Then my presence must confuse them," he said.

Mollow pursed her thin lips. "I am not so sure. I think—"

One of the Oiskins, evidently the hunt leader, brandished his spear and shouted something. Allie looked to Mollow for a translation.

"He thinks you are one of them," she said. "He wonders what happened to your hair."

Instinctively Allie rubbed a hand over his face, feeling the whiskers he had left unattended for well over a day. "Chemo," he said.

She scowled. "What?"

"Nothing. Bad joke. It looks like he wants us to join him up there."

"I do not think we have a choice, unless I change. And I do not think I should do that, except under duress."

Allie let her lead the way; this was her territory, and she knew it far better. When they reached the top of the embankment, the Oiskins separated them. Two in the lead bracketed Mollow, while the two in back guarded Allie. The fifth Oiskin led the way over the uneven, blue-grass-covered terrain. From time-to-time Allie stumbled and was struck with a spear. Mollow, however, seemed to be treated well. He wondered what he had done to fall into disfavor.

Soon they reached a sparsely wooded area, beyond which lay a rude encampment. Allie counted half a dozen males and females then stopped counting. One of the Oiskins escorting him now began to bark his back with the spear every five steps or so. Allie forced himself to tolerate this treatment, at least until he learned what was going on. Had the Oiskin who had taken shelter with him and Mollow reported them to his chief? If so, why?

"They think you are one of them," Mollow said, without looking back at him. "To them you are an aberration…no, that is not the right word."

"I don't understand," Allie said, as he was struck again by the spear.

They entered the encampment. Mollow was ushered away by a trio of Oiskin females, while Allie was made to sit against a tree. A fibrous rope was brought to secure him to the tree. After his captors had poked him several times with the butts of their spears, they left him alone.

Mollow had been led off to the far side of the encampment, there to be surrounded by males and females. Several of them gesticulated at her and made gruff sounds Allie interpreted as derisive or insulting. One of the males shook his spear at her. Allie tried to shift position—his left buttock was on top of a hard and sharp stone—and succeeded only in drawing attention to himself. Another prod of a spear suggested he was not to move.

Presently a dozen males armed with spears gathered before Allie, standing some ten paces away. By gesture and by the way they held their spears, it was clear to him they meant to cast them at him. He struggled to free his arms from the rope that held him to the tree. As he squirmed his lower body in futility, the males laughed at him. Finally one Oiskin shifted his hold on a spear, and made ready to cast it, as if he had won the right to go first. A rock hurled by a young Oiskin male struck him just above the left ear, and darkness fell on the world of perpetual light.

~ * ~

The first emotion Allie felt when he regained consciousness was surprise. This was short-lived, for Mollow was standing beside him, cutting at his bonds. Liberated, he struggled to his feet, steadying himself against Mollow. He looked around; there was not an Oiskin in sight.

His throat was parched. "What," he began, and summoned enough saliva to swallow. "What happened?" he croaked.

"They regarded you as an abomination," she said, holding him up as they walked from the encampment. "Because you defiled yourself with me. You were to be executed; I was to be eaten."

"I really don't understand."

"Oiskin means 'men.' By implication, anyone not Oiskin is not a man."

"Or woman," Allie asked.

"They do not count. No, they related to you as Oiskin, but you violated a taboo. As far as they were concerned, I was part of their diet."

Allie stammered. "That's...but that's..."

"That is the way it is. Do you wish to go back or go on?"

"I want to see this land," he replied. "I'm going to be here the rest of my life."

"That is a sensible attitude."

"How did you save me?" he asked.

They reached a fork in the river. The main current slipped off to the left, and a creek curved to the right. They followed the creek. From time to time, Allie spotted little splashes in the water, as if some creatures lived there. Now that they had traveled past the Oiskin encampment, the trees had thinned, and they began to cross a land riven with washes and covered with blue and violet vegetation, some of which yielded white flowers. Mollow plucked a few buds, tore off the petals, and gave them to Allie.

"There is not much nutrition," she said, "but the flavor is delightful."

He chewed thoughtfully. "Like peppermint chocolate," he decided.

Amused, she hissed. "I would not know. Allie, to answer your question. The Oiskin do not know that we Alassal can change shape. They never see us change. When they invade our moiety, they find creatures they did not expect. In order for me to rescue you, I had to change to a fearsome creature. They witnessed this. I hope that, in their terror, they did not realize what had happened."

"Mollow, will you be in trouble?"

She shook her head. "I think it was inevitable the Oiskin should discover our ability. But this does change things."

"I'm sorry."

She nuzzled the side of his neck. "It was not your fault." She led him to the right. "Let us cross here," she said. "The wash is shallow."

"Whose moiety is this?" he asked.

"A fair question. It is claimed by the Oiskin and," she pointed at a distant forest, "the Lannar who live there. That is where we are headed."

"Lannar?" Allie said, after a minute or so passed without explanation.

Mollow hissed and shook her head, as if the question were irrelevant; they were, after all, going to arrive soon, which would provide answers.

"They are rather like you," she said at last. "They study the land and the water and the air. Their skin is…like that of your companion, only lighter."

"Companion? You mean Thadie? We came here together, that's all." In a light whisper, he added, "I don't think she likes me."

"Yes, I understand the words 'like' and 'love.' As you use them, they express emotions of favoritism. Or they can be used negatively. We do not use them in reference to one another. We are only just beginning to understand how you apply them."

Allie had no response to this.

"We watch or listen to your transmissions, when we can, to explain to us your relationships. My favorite is *General Hospital*."

Allie choked, then coughed.

"It is so confusing that it is a challenge to interpret it," Mollow went on. "And some of your transmissions are of lands and waters we have never seen. There is a series called *Planet Earth*, and another called *Blue Planet*." She looked downcast. "One day I would like to see this. But of course I never can."

Again he did not know what to say.

In silence they traveled. With no measure of time to relate to, he had to gauge the passing of it by how he felt physically. The terrain began to change; it was less rugged, with fewer washes, and even those were shallow. At least, he thought, there was no sun beating down on them. Still, it was hot enough to draw perspiration. He lifted the front of his shirt to wipe his forehead.

A smear of blue in the distance proved to be a forest. He could just make out movement in it. When they closed to within fifty yards or so, Mollow pointed to the people and said, "There. Do you see?"

"They seem to recognize you," he said, as they came within a dozen paces of them. "But I don't think they are pleased to see me."

"They are merely curious." As an after-thought, she added, "It is said Abner Perry once passed this way. Perhaps he failed to make a favorable impression on them."

Unlike the Alassals, who had structures but preferred the freedom and comfort of tree branches, the Lannars built homes of stone and fired brick. As the kiln was on the bank of the creek, Allie concluded a great deposit of clay was nearby. The roofs consisted of a framework over which sheaves of grass had been placed. This would leak during rainstorms, but overall provide sufficient protection.

As Mollow approached, one of the Lannar females stepped forward to greet her in a language Allie did not understand. Mollow introduced her as Iskandar. Like the other members of her moiety, her skin was dusky violet in color, halfway in tone between his and Thadie's. Her height, however, was almost equal to his. Like the other males and females, she was wearing a wraparound skirt of animal skin, and nothing else. Clearly the Lannar females nursed their young. At first, Allie found himself averting his eyes from her, but her frown suggested this might be discourteous.

After Mollow introduced him, Iskandar switched to English. "We have heard there was someone from Above." She placed her spread hand—like his, it had four digits and an opposable thumb, but all webbed to the first knuckle—flat between her breasts, and waited, eyeing him carefully. After he responded in the same manner, she smiled. "You are welcome on our grass, Allie. Would you care for some water?"

Expecting him to follow, she turned and went into the encampment, making her way directly toward one of the huts. It had open doorways and windows, but no door or glazing. When he hesitated at the doorway, she beckoned him inside. Mollow pointedly did not follow, but moved off to another hut, where she was greeted by a Lannar she knew.

007: Glimmer

Iskandar poured a viscous yellow liquid into two bowls of fired clay. With a stick from the hearth, she set fire to the liquid lighting the interior of the hut. There was just the one room, its walls lined with shelves stocked with jars, vases, and wooden boxes with lids. One of the shelves bore a few stacks of parchments, and even from three paces away and in the dim light Allie could make out some form of writing on them. At the end of the shelves stood a low wooden table bearing what looked like a monitor screen. For a few seconds Allie stood frozen, staring at it in disbelief, before moving.

Along a windowless wall stood two braces of mortared brick topped by sheets of wood bound together with rope. On top of the wood was a long pad for sleeping consisting of animal skins sewn together and stuffed with some soft substance. Bemused, Iskandar watched while Allie examined it. The animals who had contributed their skins must have been almost human in size; he had yet to see live ones, but evidently they were around somewhere. A gesture from Iskandar invited him to sit down if he wished, and he did so.

In his growing awareness of her naked upper body, he averted his eyes from her. A moment later, he recognized that this avoidance was part of the emotional baggage Gullaf had mentioned. Iskandar was casually natural in her appearance, oblivious to his notice. With a bit of difficulty he managed to alter his interpretation; this, like many other things in this subcrustal world, would require getting used to.

With that knowledge settled into his mind, he was able to view Iskandar as the person she was, and not the object she might be. In his eyes now, she became much more than her appearance. In that way, she filled a niche inside him he had not realized existed. She was —could be—a friend, a relationship far more difficult to achieve than the sexual.

From a terracotta pitcher she filled a glazed cup with water and brought it to him. She did not sit down.

Hesitant to accept the cup from her, he asked, "Is this a ceremony I should know about?"

The corners of her mouth turned up in an amused smile. "Do

you mean, if you accept this water, are we mated?"

Allie tried not to laugh. The way she said it made him feel ridiculous. "Well...something like that, I guess. I'm sorry, I don't mean—"

"I think I understand." After he took the cup and drank from it, she sat down beside him. "No, we do not mate in the manner we see from your transmissions. We are not invasive like you. When it is time for me to...to..." Her dark face twisted. "I do not know this word. To bring forth an egg."

"Ovulate?"

She tasted the word on her tongue, and nodded, and he knew she had filed the word away for future reference.

"To ovulate, yes, thank you, I shall share this word. When it is time for me to ovulate, I bring the egg forth and place it in the water and secure it so it will not float away. I will then select a male, who will cause his seed to be ejected onto it. After a time, a small one of us will have formed...if the infants we see on your transmissions are accurate, this small one would be about half that size. We see to its feeding in the water, where it stays until it is able to crawl forth. At that time, we determine whether it is female or male—not that it makes a difference the way we see it does in your transmissions—and I will commence nursing it to supplement its diet until it is able to acquire sustenance on its own."

"I suppose there will be a quiz," he murmured.

"A quiz?" Abruptly she laughed. "Oh! Oh, yes, a quiz. A test. No, Allie. You led into this subject with questions you clearly did not know how to form. I answered them. Is this not so?"

He gathered himself. "So people from Above would not mate with you."

"It would be pointless." Her deep purple eyes narrowed, and he realized she had acquired several words of body language from the transmissions. "Did you wish to mate with me in your way?"

He drew back an inch or two and looked away.

"I have presented you with a quandary," Iskandar apologized. "If you respond that you do wish it, you fear I will accept. If you decline, as is your true wish, you fear being discourteous."

"Something like that," he admitted.

Tenderly she touched his arm. "It is our sleep time. Mollow brought you to me to be my guest for sleeping. You are under my roof, and you have drunk my water. Like any of us would be in this

circumstance, for such is our way, you are therefore under my protection and may avail yourself of my comfort."

"It has been a long trek to get here," he said.

"And you are tired. I shall be here until you sleep, and I shall be
here when you awaken." Gently she nudged him onto the pad and
stretched out beside him. "Sleep now."

~ * ~

Allie had no idea just how fatigued he had been until he awoke
feeling utterly refreshed. Awoke to a pair of purple eyes glistening in
the flames from the oil lamps as she gazed down at him. She neither
smiled nor frowned, but gave a tiny nod.

"Whenever I visit another moiety," she said, "I too feel out of
place, and this tires me. It is not surprising you slept for so long."

He tried to sit up, but her hand on his chest stopped him. For a
moment he wondered whether there was more to this process of
waking up. "Iskandar, no."

"Whenever you wish, if you wish." She got up, and he sat up.
"We shall eat first," she told him. "Then it will be time for us to go."

That both puzzled and startled him. "Go where?" Tendons
spoke as he stretched his legs out. "Wait. For *us* to go?"

"You do wish to continue your journey, do you not?"

"But Mollow…"

"She will soon return to her moiety. This is as far as she is able
to go. You are my charge now."

She handed him a terracotta dish of what looked like jerked meat
and dried fruit. He tried the fruit first; it tasted rather like manioc,
but the texture was more like caramel. He held up a chunk of jerky.
"What did this come from?"

Iskandar gave him a blank expression, as if she expected him to
already know. "We call the creature a *deekabos*. It is a…" She paused,
searching for a word. "For you, it would be between a wildebeest
and a steer from your cowboy movies." She made a face. "I think."

"I have much to learn," he muttered.

"In that regard, I will not dispute you." She hesitated. "May I
ask?"

He finished chewing. "Of course."

"Why are you on this trek?"

Allie considered. *Why, indeed?* In the back of his mind there might have been, on and off, a vague notion of returning to the surface—a move he clearly and consciously knew to be impossible. But what if, what if? True, he wanted to see this subcrustal world for its own sake—if for no other reason than he was stuck here and it made sense to know what "here" was. But what if?

And how should he respond to Iskandar?

The truth shall set you free, he thought. He liberated himself.

"Maybe I'll find a way back up," he said. He kept his tone casual as he asked, "Perhaps you know of or have heard of a way."

Her long hesitation sent shivers up his spine and made his heart pound. Her eyes met his shoulder, the open doorway, the coals in the hearth, but they did not meet his own eyes.

"Iskandar?" he whispered.

Still she would not look at him; she scarcely seemed to breathe.

Hands clenched to stones Allie turned away. He wanted to strike out in frustration, but not at her. A tree outside the hut beckoned, and he went out and banged his fist against it, once, twice, thrice, and blood began to ooze from a small gash on the edge of his hand.

The touch on his shoulder immediately drained him of all violence. He turned back around. She was weeping. "Do not," she told him, choked.

He tried a wan smile. "The tree felt nothing."

She took up his hand. "But you are bleeding. Come back inside."

A Lannar male waved to her in greeting; she gave a desultory wave back, but she looked only at Allie now as she led him into her hut. He came willingly, ashamed of his outburst. She drew him to the bed and sat him down. From a shelf she gathered a clay vial and a fragment of tanned skin and joined him on the bed. The contents of the vial stung like alcohol, though they appeared to be some kind of plant oil. She pressed the skin against the wound and held it there. Now her eyes met his. He saw the reflection of his face in them.

It was easy to read too much into the care she was giving him. Were she a human woman, an interlude and perhaps a bonding might well be in the offing. But his interpretation was human; she, was not. Or so he had to keep telling himself. With her this close, much of him remained unconvinced.

"Thank you," he said.

"You are under my roof and have drunk my water."

"Yes. Iskandar…"

She sat back, taking his hint under consideration. For a long moment she said nothing, nor did she give any indication she was about to speak. Her gaze was fixed on something across the room. When at last she did speak, her voice was barely audible, though it came from a distance of less than two feet.

"It is said Abner Perry spent his life here Below, searching for a way out. He found nothing. If you wish, I will take you to the site of his grave—he wanted to be buried, you see."

Allie waited, holding his breath, waiting for her to continue, for surely she had something more to say on the matter.

"There was a man named David," she went on. "He stayed with several moieties, including ours. I cannot say how long ago this was; I never met him. This was before I set foot on land. One day he did not return from his adventures. Some say he was killed, and his body consumed by scavengers. Others say he…he found a way out. A way back to Above."

"And…what do you believe, Iskandar?"

She drew a little breath. "I can only tell you the direction in which he was headed when he departed for the last time. But there is danger in the land we will have to travel." She looked down at her hands, folded in her lap. "There is one other consideration," she whispered.

"And that would be?"

She twisted on the bed to face him. "If we find a way out, take me with you."

Allie did not respond directly. "If we should find it, I will have to return to the Alassals to bring Thadie with me, if she wants to come."

"She is your…?"

"She came with me by accident, but as a result of something I was trying to do."

"Then she is someone you would wave to upon seeing."

Allie chuckled. "I suppose you could say it that way." Inside, he was asking himself whether Iskandar had understated the relationship. He found himself wondering about Thadie, and her sojourn with the Alassals. He and she had survived a harrowing experience. It was only natural this would form some sort of emotional bond between them. The truth was he missed her, even her snarky tones and bitter attitude.

"Perhaps more than wave to," Iskandar said softly.

"Do you watch a lot of our television?" he asked her.

"I am not certain it is healthy to do so."

A broad grin tugged at his mouth. "Many of us have said that very thing."

For a long time Iskandar was silent. Her unfocused eyes indicated a pause for reflection. But they were also clouded over; curtains now hung over the windows into her soul. Allie himself began to let his own thoughts drift. Inevitably he drew comparisons between Mollow and Iskandar. Aside from physical differences, where the Alassal was nonchalant about what he considered intimate activities, Iskandar appeared to take them more seriously. They meant something to her, even if only as expressions of roofing. He recalled the Bedouins had a similar rule in their culture. One who has eaten their bread and slept under their roof was protected by the host from harm from outside; by a blood feud supported by the entire tribe, if it should come to that.

Roofing, he thought. The Lannars saw to the safety and comfort of their guests. As security, the roof was inviolate. Now her eyes seemed to clear, a rich, glistening amethyst in the last flickers of the oil lamps, and once more she saw him. A faint smile said she was happy to find him still with her.

She stood up and stepped toward some shelves. "I had better pack a few things," she told him. Looking over her shoulder, she eyed him carefully. "Have you nothing to bring with you?"

"There is only my backpack," he replied, toeing it where it lay on the floor.

"Have you any weapons?"

"A small knife. Nothing else."

Her hand rummaged around inside a rawhide pouch the size of the average purse. "Ah," she said—and withdrew a revolver.

Utterly astonished, Allie could only gape at her as she brought it to him. It seemed to be lightly coated with the same oil she had used to burn for illumination. His military training stepped to the fore. He broke open the cylinder and counted four live rounds and two empty casings. After extracting all six—they appeared to be .45 caliber—he closed the cylinder and tested the action. Checking the weapon, he realized there was no safety.

"Do you know how to use this?" Iskandar asked him.

"More importantly, I know when to use it," he said. "And when not to. Have you any more of these rounds?"

She brought him a pouch with a tie string. The contents clicked metallically. He opened the pouch and counted to seven.

"It was said these were in a container," she explained. "The container dissolved long ago."

"Probably cardboard or card paper," he said. "This is a very old weapon."

"Do you think it will work?"

"I should fire a test round," he said. "But not here. The noise might frighten people." After reloading he tucked the pistol under his belt. "Iskandar...we may be gone for a long time."

"If you are concerned for my roof, there is no need. If for food, we shall find some along the way."

Just like that, he thought. *We're leaving just like that.*

008: Any Port

"He left just like that?" Thadie gasped. "No goodbyes, no invitation to come along, no nothing?"

"I am sorry," Mollow said.

Flustered, Thadie threw up her hands. "But what am I to do?" she cried. "What…where…*why* did he leave? What was he thinking?" Her eyes narrowed. "Was he alone?"

"Iskandar was with him."

"Damn the bloody man," she snarled. "Typical white man. Always focused on his crotch." She cast a hard look at Mollow. "I don't suppose you know where they went."

"I know what was overheard," the Alassal said slowly.

Thadie resisted the urge to throttle her. "Tell me!"

"It is a delusion. I believe I use that word correctly. Your Allie is looking for a way back to Above. There are legends and rumors of such a path, but no one has been able to confirm them or to find such a place. But there are sources of information one might approach. Such information may be heeded only at peril. But Iskandar is leading him to one such source. It is the same source David was supposed to have used."

"David? Who is this David?"

"No one now knows. He was said to have come from Above. There was no television for us at that time—or for you, for that matter. He was said to have searched for a way Above…and he disappeared. No one knows where he went or what happened to him. This was long ago, before my hatching. He is surely dead now, even if he is still here Below."

"This is very frustrating, Mollow."

"I am sorry. It is the way it is."

"We have a saying like that Above as well." Thadie considered briefly. "Mollow, do you know where they might have gone?"

"I…think so."

"Can you take me there?"

"It is perilous."

"Yes. Life is like that. Will you take me there?"

The hesitation that followed lasted long enough to annoy Thadie. She was about to turn away when the Alassal said, "If that is what you wish, I will do so. But I must caution you that you may not like what you find, if you find it at all."

"I don't know what that means," Thadie said.

"It means that—"

"Mollow, I don't care what it means. I want to find Allie."

The Alassal patted her belly. "Then I shall pack some food for us."

"And weapons."

"No. We shall have no need for them."

~ * ~

Following the route Mollow had taken earlier with Allie, she and Thadie crossed the bridge and made their way over terrain riven by gullies and washes. Unlike the previous route, however, Mollow soon set a course for a line of blue-violet mountains along the horizon. Thadie estimated the distance at fifty miles, or two days' journey at a minimum—assuming the mountains were the destination. Mollow was unhelpful, and restricted her conversation to the necessary. The silence discomfited Thadie, even though she herself was hardly talkative. She had the impression that for some reason Mollow did not approve of the journey they were taking. The Alassal was not concerned about danger, and she had said nothing about impassable terrain. So what was it, then?

Although the temperature had not altered perceptibly, Thadie was beginning to perspire from the effort of the trek. Mollow had stored some water in her pouch, with the assurance they would find more water along the way, but it was not yet time for a break. Thadie kept walking. Light from the great overhead cast her shadow. She missed the sun. Out of the forest, the air was thinner. None of the plants (Allie would have called them plantanalogs) looked familiar. Now and then something scurried past her feet for cover. She wondered whether there were spiders in the area. She wondered why Allie had gone off on his own, without her.

She and he had hardly spoken with one another since their arrival at the Alassal moiety. She had to admit she did not readily invite conversation. She knew about Ssakileh; perhaps there was also something between him and Mollow. Why he should desire any such relationship with either female was beyond her.

A rumble in the air brought Mollow to a stop, with Thadie catching her up. Both of them looked at the sky. Dark clouds had already gathered, to be sliced up by lightning. Thadie had already survived one flood; she did not look forward to another.

"How long?" she asked Mollow.

She gestured in the direction they had been going. "We can make that small forest," she said. "But we must avoid the washes; they fill quickly."

With nothing more to be discussed, they picked up their pace. The peals of thunder encouraged them in this. Raindrops began to fall just as they reached the shelter of the trees.

They hurried further into the forest. Here the terrain was more rugged, and uneven, with the roots of some trees protruding from the banks of the washes. Rain began to pelt through the foliage above. Mollow appeared to be searching for something as they gradually slowed down. Finally she gave a little hiss of satisfaction and led Thadie to a raised embankment where a great tree had fallen. There was a shelter of sorts caused by the evacuation of the earth where the root system had been. They crept under it and struggled for comfortable positions. Water dripped from the overhanging roots; some of it reached them, but they had already squirmed to the back of the cavity.

Beginning to shiver, her parchment shift damp, Thadie hugged herself. Mollow held out an arm, the invitation implicit. Thadie shook her head almost violently. A thin tendril, like a warm noodle, penetrated her mind for a second or two.

Mollow spoke gently. "I mean you no harm, nor do I wish to bring shame to you. You are chilled. We will both be warmer if we sit closer together."

The trees shook with the thunder. Thadie drew herself up to Mollow, and together they huddled against the storm.

009: Friendly Persuasion

The path Iskandar chose took them across terrain even more rugged and broken than that which he had passed on the way to the Lannar settlement. Dirt yielded under his boots, and several times Iskandar had to steady him to prevent him from falling into a gully. In the distance, to their righ,t a great storm had gathered, the dark and light gray clouds swirling like a swarm. A great gray wall indicated a torrential downpour.

"Will that reach us?" he asked. The memory of a recent flood washed over him, and he could still taste the mud in his mouth.

Iskandar watched it for long seconds. "No. It will empty itself, and fade. There will be flooding, but these gullies will not fill."

He looked around. "That's good. Because I see no shelter for us anywhere."

She pointed toward a clutch of foothills. "If we must, we can take refuge there."

Allie squinted into the distance. The hills, by his estimation, were five miles away. Another two hours, at minimum. He had the impression the land itself was ever so slightly uphill. He shrugged his backpack into a more comfortable position and followed in Iskandar's footsteps.

Although there was no wind, several yards off to his left a shrub was moving back and forth. At the base of it rested a dark shape. Hand on the butt of the pistol, Allie kept his eye on it. The shape shifted just a little, and he could make out a head at one end of it. If it had a tail, it was curled up tight. Overall its size was that of a bear cub. In the shadow of the shrub, a pair of intense green eyes glowed as if they were radioactive. The creature seemed to be eyeing Allie in the same way he regarded it: watchful, wary.

"Iskandar?" he said softly.

"I see it. It has fed. It is no threat."

Quickly he glanced around. "Fed? What does it eat?"

"Whatever it wants."

Still looking back at it, Allie took a wrong step. As the ground gave way and he began to spill into the wash, he felt Iskandar's hand snag his forearm. But the momentum of his falling carried her with him, and together they tumbled onto the sand a couple meters below. Laughing.

"Are you all right?" he gasped, sitting up.

Iskandar brushed sand from her body. "Perhaps I should find an easier trail for us," she said. "But this is the only one I know."

"I'm really sorry. I should watch where I'm going."

He got to his feet and extended a hand to her, to help her up. She took it and rose, and he found himself standing within a scant inch or two of her. Warmth suffused him. Whether from her proximity or from within himself, he could not say; probably it came from both.

He stepped back. "I'll be more careful," he promised, and looked up. "How do we get out of here?"

"There may be a way further along the wash," she suggested, turning to head in that direction. After two paces, he caught her up.

The only sounds now were the chuffing of their feet on the sand, and the intermittent breaths they drew and expelled. The wash wound past several dark outcrops that he recognized as basaltic. A few plants, some with small blue flowers, struggled along the base of the walls. It occurred to him that considerable time had passed since water had filled the wash. To him, that suggested changes in climate, this despite the relative stability of the temperature and the weather. A sound reached him as he was deep in thought. Blinking, he brought himself back up.

"What was that?" he asked her.

"I merely noted you were distracted. You are distracted, are you not?"

"I am still getting to know this land."

The growth on the low hills gradually resolved itself into a forest. Even from three miles away Allie could see the trunks were misshapen, as if they had been twisted by high winds from all directions. They reminded him of some of the windswept pines along the coast of southern California, except these were shorter and more massive. There appeared to be several breaks in the wall of trees. They invited entry into the depths of the forest.

The answer to Allie's question was obvious, but he asked it anyway. "Is that where we are headed?" he asked. "That opening?"

"It only appears to be an opening," Iskandar told him. "A tree is missing. A flood undercut it, and it tumbled into the wash. Do you see the opening to the right?"

It hardly looked wide enough to qualify. "Yeah," Allie replied, but he offered no opinion.

"The grave of Abner Parry is in there, halfway up the slope," she reminded him. "It is said David wished to see it. After he disappeared, it was not said whether he had visited the site."

Already Allie had grasped much of the story, but the last sentence she uttered intrigued him. Could the disappearance of this David be connected in some way to whatever he had seen at the gravesite? If so, this could signify the presence of a way out, back to Above. He felt a surge of excitement, and had to tamp it back down, for it was just as likely the grave was simply a grave, without any answers.

"It is there that you may have need of the weapon I gave you," Iskandar added.

"That's comforting," he replied.

Iskandar shot him a harsh look for the sarcasm, but his flashed smile disarmed her. For a minute and more he studied the sky, especially the black clouds that continued to deluge the lands in the distance to his right. It seemed to him the sky overall was lightening, as if the storm were about to break. A sardonic nook in the back of his mind said one could make a life's career out of interpreting the weather here Below. Flash flood warnings might be especially useful.

They had walked for another ten minutes before Allie slowed his pace. "We should rest," he said. "That storm is breaking up. It won't affect us. And we've been walking for several hours now."

"I do not know your measurements of time," she said. "But I agree. There is a copse of...you might call them orangewoods, growing on that low hill. The grass will be comfortable. There is a creek beyond where I can draw water as well."

Though Iskandar had not spoken of previous journeys, her words left no doubt in Allie's mind that she had traveled this way before, perhaps more than once. As they headed for the trees—tree analogs, he had to remind himself—he wondered whether Iskandar had rested here previously. Certainly, as they drew nearer, it looked like a good spot.

With anticipation still lurking in its dark nook, Allie found himself wishing Thadie were with him. Racial discord aside, she was...

He was unable to complete that thought. She and he had

traveled a brief but frightening and arduous journey together, during which—so he thought—there had at least been some minor bonding of a friendly nature. But she was, and probably had always been, fully aware of differences in skin color, where he had always held to King's dream of judgment by character. Here, in a land where a multiplicity of races—species? —coexisted, he had seen no evidence so far that a people, such as the Oiskins, was disliked for any reason save their behavior. Where relations festered incessantly Above, King's dream seemed to rule Below.

"You are deep in thought," Iskandar said.

They had arrived at the orangewoods without his awareness of that fact. After slipping off his backpack, he immediately sat down on soft grass and leaned back against the tree. It had just occurred to him, while he considered attitudes toward race, that as much as he would like to return to Above, he was ready to accept remaining in Below. But Iskandar had said he might need the pistol she gave him.

She jostled him as she sat down beside him. Together they gazed toward the dissipating storm, the rolling land that stretched between, and the dry wash nearby. He wished they had planned a picnic and brought a six-pack. Belatedly he realized he had seen no sign of alcoholic beverages among the peoples he had already visited. Still, drinking beer was no reason for him to return to the surface.

He was about to make some comment when she anticipated him, and made a little hissing sound accompanied by a movement of her flat hand up and down. She then pointed at something beyond their feet. Vaguely understanding, Allie kept silent. Presently the grass a couple yards away began to quiver with the passage of some small animal. Allie briefly watched a violet triangular head move toward him, followed by a sinuous, furry body. Without the fur, which was also violet, he might have thought the creature was a snake. When it drew within a few inches of Allie's outstretched legs, it paused and raised its head about a foot above the grass. Two bright green eyes seemed to assess him.

"Make no sound or movement," Iskandar whispered.

That order wrapped coils of tension around Allie's entire body. Was the creature dangerous, venomous? Or was it simply skittish, ready to flee at the slightest suggestion of a threat? He kept very still. The creature leaned closer to Allie's booted feet and seemed to be sniffing them. Tension mounted within him; he wanted to roll away, but dared not do so. A little nudge against the toe of his boot forced him to stifle a cry of alarm.

Finally the creature pulled away, though it did not lower its head as it turned it toward Iskandar. It emitted faint squeaking noises. Iskandar's reply in the same sort of sounds made the hair on the back of Allie's neck and shoulders rustle under his collar.

"She says you are too big to eat," Iskandar said.

Words momentarily failed Allie. He only managed, "That... that's good to know." He pointedly did not ask whether she or the creature was serious. "You—you can speak with it?"

"Yes, of course. Every living thing has its own language, does it not? Including this woegong here."

Long lumps formed at either side of the woegong's neck. These slowly extended to short arms and hands, which it held out toward Iskandar in supplication. She fished around in her carrybag and withdrew a smaller bag secured with a drawstring. From it, she removed a reddish-brown object about the size of a cockroach. This she held out to the woegong, who snatched it from her hand and began to gnaw on it.

"Those are roasted firlins...you might call them cockroaches," Iskandar said. "The woegongs regard them as a delicacy."

"Did you expect to encounter one of these woegongs along the way?" he asked.

She shook her head. "Not at all. I find firlins quite palatable, although they do tend to stick between the teeth. But they are high in protein and fat."

The woegong held out its hands for another.

"Strange world," Allie sighed, shaking his head.

"No stranger than yours," Iskandar replied. She gave the woegong another firlin, and they watched the creature slither away.

"Yeah," Allie agreed. "Evolution followed similar lines, but definitely not the same ones. I feel out of place, Iskandar."

She shook her head. "You have drunk my water, and you are with me. That is your place, at least for now."

He twisted on the grass to face her. "For now?"

She looked away. "We cannot know what will be," she said. "We can only hope to be ready for what will be."

"As Below, so Above."

A smile flickered uncertainly on her face. "What does that

mean?"

"We're not so different, Iskandar, you and I," he said. "Above, we prepare for the future, but we don't know exactly what it will be. We can only be as ready as we can. And when the future arrives, it is always somewhat different from what we expected. I imagine that's true here as well...Iskandar, what do you call all this?" His arm swept around him. "All this land, what do you call it?"

The question seemed to confuse her. She shook herself as if trying to clear away a mist. "We do not," she began, and stopped. "It is not...there is no name that we use. There are only moieties. Alassal, Oiskin, and Lannar, as you know. These moieties, and others, regard this as Below."

"Others?" he asked.

"Yes, of course, others. Just as you have Above, do you not?"

"Not...quite," he said. "Whether our moiety is American, or German, or Japanese, or Zulu, we are all the same species. We can mate and produce offspring. That is not true here."

There was no rancor in her tone when she said, "You humans are very concerned with mating. But not you," she added quickly. "At least, you have not behaved as they do on your television programs."

"Television," he laughed.

Her eyes narrowed. "Are you then concerned with mating?"

"There is a time and a place for it, Iskandar."

"Such passion. That is the right word, is it not? Passion?"

He grinned. "There are interludes."

"Yes. As with Mollow."

Now Allie started. "You know about that?"

"And with Ssakileh. Mollow told me."

"How...when did she tell you? I never saw you speak with her."

"While you were sleeping. I did not wish to awaken you. You looked so peaceful. Allie, was it supposed to be a secret, you and Ssakileh and Mollow?"

"No, not at all, but..." Unaccustomed to common knowledge of intimate relationships, he found himself unable to complete the sentence.

"It is a strange world, Above," Iskandar said.

"And Below," he said, and started to rise. "We should push on."

Iskandar did not budge. "We may rest here," she said. "It is comfortable. And the grave will still be there when we reach it. Sleep now."

Iskandar stretched out on the grass and pulled Allie down alongside her. Presently the woegong returned, and joined them.

010: Getting to Know You

The storm broke, as all storms do eventually. Thadie found herself drifting in wakefulness, random thoughts like sparks of lightning showing her the way then leaving her in the dark. Beside her, Mollow slept on, oblivious to the changes in Thadie's respiration.

The drip of water from the lip of the overhang slowed to a trickle and stopped altogether. The light from the lining of crystal far overhead increased as the clouds vanished. For Thadie, Below was like living inside a geode. This world was the empty space, covered on the top side by luminescent crystal and on the bottom, where she was, by land. A sardonic smile crossed her lips as she hoped no gigantic gem collector took a lapidary saw to the place.

She sat up, jostling Mollow, who awoke instantly. "Is something amiss?" she asked, her face brightening to its customary mahogany color. Quickly she looked around, as if on the verge of changing her shape to that of a fearsome creature in defense of its lair and of her guest.

"I'm just thinking," Thadie said. "Nothing in particular. Just thinking. The rain has stopped."

"Are you hungry?"

"Not very. We should go."

Gingerly they climbed from under the great tree roots. After a moment or two of reorientation, Mollow made a little gesture, and they headed off once again for the distant mountains. The air around them was dank and humid, and again Thadie's body was soon slick with perspiration. Mollow, on the other hand, was protected by scales, and seemed to revel in the heat. Thadie considered that; but if the Alassals were cold-blooded, it had not affected the warmth Thadie had received from Mollow as they slept. It's a whole different evolution down here, Allie had told her; she had no doubt of that.

They crossed a rough patch of terrain strewn with briars. These had no effect on Mollow, but Thadie's bare lower legs were soon etched with naughts-and-crosses. Most of the scratches were simply red, but a few released drops of blood now and then. Seeing this, Mollow came to a halt at a smooth patch of sand and pebbles.

From her pouch Mollow extracted a small bag made of pale brown parchment and undid the drawstring. "Sit down, please," she told Thadie.

Thadie complied. Mollow seated herself at Thadie's feet and drew one of her legs onto her lap. From the bag she extracted a clear vial of a viscous blue liquid. She dipped a fingertip into the liquid and began to trace the red lines on Thadie's leg. A sharp intake of breath over her teeth was Thadie's only concession to the stings. One leg treated, Mollow worked on the other. When she was finished, Thadie's lower legs were cross-hatched in royal blue. After a few seconds the liquid cooled her wounds and ceased to sting.

"There will be no infection," Mollow said, tightening the drawstring and tucking the bag back into her pouch. "How does it feel?"

"Better," said Thadie. "Much better. Thank you."

They resumed walking. The terrain roughened again, and this time it supported low spreading blue plants with tiny white flowers reminiscent in shape of Maltese crosses. Thadie stooped to pick one, without adverse effect, although she realized belatedly as she rose with it she should have asked Mollow whether it was safe to touch. The flower emitted a sweet aroma, rather like jasmine at night.

"So many plants are blue here," she said, mostly to herself.

"It is due to a copper-based pigment that absorbs light from the crystals you see above you," Mollow explained. "Yellow is another common color."

"The grass on the slope where we first landed was variegated, blue with yellow edging."

Mollow's tone contained a shrug. "There are other colors, too."

"So much to learn," Thadie mused.

"And to unlearn. But it is easier if you are open to it."

Thadie glanced at her sharply. "What does *that* mean?"

Mollow spoke with some hesitation. "It is not my place to say."

They reached the bank of a shallow wash before Thadie could pursue this. For several paces they walked along the edge, with Mollow looking for a way down that both she and Thadie would be able to descend. Finally she settled on a steep slope. With a warning to step carefully, she began her descent. It was only five or six feet to the bottom of the wash, but the rock was friable and offered little purchase for her feet. Finally, exasperated, she dropped the last four feet or so to the sand below.

"Now you," she called up to Thadie.

She took a step back from the edge. "You mean…you mean jump down?" She shook her head violently. "I—I can't!"

"Of course you can," Mollow said calmly. "I will catch you."

"I'll fall."

"I will hold you up." With a trace of impatience she added, "We have to cross this; there is no other way. And…" She paused, keening an ear. "Now, Thadie! Jump!"

Thadie leaped out and landed with stiffened knees. Staggering, her knees painfully jarred, she just managed, with Mollow's support, to remain upright.

"What's that sound?" Thadie asked.

It had begun as a soft rumble and grown into a roar. Even as they looked in the direction of the sound, they saw it: a great wall of frothy water almost as high as the wash banks.

Thadie's heart pounded. She recalled her earlier experience with a rush of water. Together they ran toward the other bank and tried to scrabble up. The rock and dirt gave way under their feet. The wall of water rushed them. Mollow caught a foothold and thrust upward, spilling the top half of her body onto the bank. Thadie's cry of terror was all but lost in the roar of the water. Mollow slung her body sideways so she was fully atop the bank. Then she reached down and caught one of Thadie's flailing arms just as the water smashed into her. Just as she screamed.

Three fingers and a thumb clutched Thadie's forearm. The impact and Thadie's weight threatened to drag her along with the flood. A fallen tree tumbled past, barely missing her as she fought to bring her free hand up to Mollow's arm. The water tore at her parchment gown and swept her legs off the wash bed. Still Mollow clung to her forearm. The drag on Thadie's body threatened to pull Mollow off the bank and into the torrent.

"Don't drop me!" Thadie screamed.

"Never!"

"Mollow…"

"Do not fight the water flow," she said suddenly. "Let it sweep you up, like you were swimming. When you are near the top of the bank, just roll onto it."

"That's," she began, and got a mouthful of muddy water. "Impossible," she burbled.

"Yes. Just do it. You have to relax your body."

"I—I…"

"Take a deep breath and relax," Mollow said, just over the sound of the water.

Thadie coughed and choked. But she relaxed in Mollow's grip. The water flow swept her to horizontal and lifted her just as Mollow said it would do. Her body slammed against the top of the bank and knocked the air out of her. For a moment she felt weak. What had Mollow said? Roll onto the bank? She could not see it. She could only feel it. She rolled, and Mollow tugged at her arm dragging her onto the bank.

Both of them collapsed on the sparse grass, gasping for air which refused to come fast enough. Mollow still had hold of Thadie's forearm. Thadie was scarcely aware of the ache of the grip. She coughed, spat, and vomited gritty water onto the grass. Her parchment gown was torn in places, and darker now that it was sodden. With her free hand she tried to tug the hem down to her knees and succeeded only in tearing loose a fragment of the garment. All the while, Mollow held onto her arm.

"I think," Thadie gasped, still coughing, "you can let go now."

Mollow released her, adding an apology. "I was frightened for you."

"I was frightened for me, too." Gradually her respiration returned to normal, and her stomach stopped lurching. "Thank you," she whispered.

Mollow's tone contained a shrug. "You are in my care."

Thadie did not know what to say to that. She gazed out at the terrain between the bank and the mountains. It now seemed as if it would take forever to cross it. If only Allie had given her the choice to accompany him, no matter which way she chose, she would not have had to embark on this journey.

"So why *am* I going?" she asked herself.

Mollow turned to her. "You are not his *ssenya*. One of his… chosen ones."

"No." She shook her head quickly. "No, no. I'm…it's complicated, and a long story, at that." She got unsteadily to her feet. "Shall we continue?"

"Do you feel strong enough?"

In response she started walking. She increased her pace after

Mollow caught her up. With the clearing of the storm, the distant mountains were a dull blue, the effect of the vegetation that covered them. The land they were crossing was a mottled blue, reflecting the hues of different species of shrubs and ground cover. Interspersed among them were yellows and even a few bright pinks.

A tiny cloud of dust brought Thadie to an immediate halt. Mollow passed her for two paces and turned back around.

"Didn't you see that?" Thadie cried. "Something just scurried across my path."

"Many creatures here scurry," Mollow said. "That was probably a *rapox*. It is harmless, unless you try to pick it up." She thought for a moment and added, "They do not taste very good."

Once more words failed Thadie. She resumed her pace, her eyes glued to the spot where the *rapox* had disappeared.

An hour and zero conversation later, the mountains discouragingly appeared no closer. Thadie asked for and got a break, sitting down on a long flat boulder. Mollow, joining her there, offered her some water, which she accepted gratefully. Thadie still had misgivings regarding the journey she had undertaken, but she gave no voice to them. It was better to leave Mollow with the impression this was important.

Mollow chose the moment to disabuse Thadie of that concern. "You do know we are telepathic, do you not?" she said. "I have read you very loosely; the changes of expression on your face tell me much more. So I must ask: why *are* you making this journey? And please, do not tell me you have asked yourself the same question. I know this much."

Thadie deftly deflected the query. "Why do you want to know? You chose to accompany me; I did not invite you."

"Had I not come along, you would now be detritus at the end of that flood. In any case, invited or not, I would have followed you."

"But why?"

"It is how we are. Even if you do not yet belong to the Alassal moiety, you are a part of it; a memory of it. None in our settlement will ever forget you or Allie."

"But…but I am human. I am not of your…your species."

"That does not signify," Mollow said. "You are the same to us. To make you feel comfortable, we took on your appearance. As Gullaf continues to do whenever he is near you." For a few seconds she gazed up at the roof of glowing crystals. "Your Allie thinks of us as he thinks of himself. He thinks of you that way as well. Yet your primary identification is that you are different. I say you are not. We are all the same," she tapped her head and her chest, "in here."

"You…you don't understand. It is *not* the same, where I come from."

"You are not where you come from," Mollow said softly.

"And he is certainly *not* my Allie."

"Then again I ask: why this journey?"

Thadie sputtered. "W-why? What…because if he finds a way out, he has to take *me*, too."

"What makes you think he would not take you?" Mollow asked, with delicate incision.

"But he…he…" Glum, she fell silent.

Having made her points, Mollow said nothing further until at last she stood up and held out an inviting hand. "There is a place we can stop for a sleep," she said. "We have some walking to do, first."

Thadie merely nodded.

011: Getting to Know All About You

Woegong was still with Allie and Iskandar when they awoke. More to the point, it was the creature's snuffling around and trying to open Iskandar's pouch containing the firlins that initially roused them. Iskandar sat up and undid the drawstring and held out a firlin, which was readily accepted.

Rummaging around in his backpack, Allie finally pulled out a granola bar, this one with chocolate chips, and unwrapped it. After taking a bite, he held it out to Iskandar, who accepted it, but hesitated.

"Did you wish to mate with me in your way?" she asked.

Allie laughed, lightly but uncertainly.

A broad smile lit her face and turned her eyes to polished amethyst. "Again you are worried about what I might think of your response." In punctuation, she took a bite, and chewing, handed the bar back to him. "It has a pleasant taste," she decided. "I do not know your word."

"Sweet?" he tried.

He ate half of what remained, and tried to pass the remainder back to her, but the woegong intercepted it. After taking a couple of nibbles, it handed the rest to Iskandar.

"I have heard this word in several meanings," she told him. "Perhaps it is what I mean now. Thank you for sharing this." With the flash of a grin, she added lightly, "Now we must mate."

Allie sighed. "Iskandar…"

"No, I understand," she went on, her tone serious now. "You have known Ssakileh and Mollow. You are not reticent on my account. But this is not what you need from me."

The woegong looked from one to the other, back and forth. At last it retreated to a spot beyond the shade of the trees, and coiled up there, with its head and neck raised, watching.

"You have made your offer plain to me, Iskandar," Allie said slowly. "And when it is time…but you see, what I need most at this time is a friend."

"I know this," she said. "And I tell you that you have a friend." She got to her feet. A little movement of her hand at her hip caused the wrap to drop to the grass. "A friend and more. Please remove your clothing now."

The woegong raised its head a little higher, as if for a better view.

~ * ~

As their trek resumed, Allie was pensive, almost to the point of distraction. He had never been aggressive in his relationships with women. When he felt an attraction, he tended to wait for the woman to make the first overt move. In that way, he was certain of what was to transpire. In that way, however, several opportunities had passed him by.

Yet he did not feel Ssakileh, Mollow, or Iskandar had been aggressive. Instead, they had behaved matter-of-factly, openly. The intimacies were significant in the moment, but not for the lifetime. There were no strings attached, and more importantly, no guilt. All that was required was consent.

"You have much to learn and unlearn, grasshopper," he muttered to himself.

Iskandar was peering into the distance. Suddenly she said, "There's a wash to our right, about ten paces away," she said, shoving him in that direction. "Hurry! Get in it and stay down."

As if sensing danger, the woegong poked its head out of her pouch to look around, but she tucked it back inside, chittering instructions at it. For his part, Allie did not question her, but dashed off. Footfalls behind him said she was following, and likely would push him into the wash if he hesitated. Clearly there was an emergency, and he had no idea what it was. But if she was frightened, then certainly he ought to be as well.

The wash was a good six feet deep and bottomed with sand. Even as he paused to gauge his leap, Iskandar pushed him. Landing, his knees buckled, and he spilled headlong onto the sand. The nearby sound of impact announced the arrival of Iskandar. Grabbing him by the backpack, she tugged him against the wall of the wash, and there they huddled.

"What?" he gasped, brushing sand from his clothing.

"And do not move," she hissed, adding a squeaked order to the woegong.

In the distance he heard what sounded like a raptor's cry. "What is it?" he whispered.

"It is one of three possible fliers…" She risked a glance over the bank. "It is a *thorga*," she replied. "You have nothing like it Above. It flies. It is not large enough to carry you off, but it can kill you and eat you where you fall. We are out in the open. It cannot get to us when we are in the forest." Briefly she studied the wash. "We will be safe enough down here," she said. "And the wash goes in the direction we want." She stood up but stayed low and took his hand. "Come. Keep down."

Crouching, they scurried over the sand and small rocks and other detritus, negotiating the bends in the wash where a bank had collapsed. Allie resisted the urge to look back; that was Iskandar's task, because she knew what to look for. At irregular intervals he heard the *thorga* cry—it sounded frustrated, though that might have been his imagination. From time-to-time Iskandar yanked him to a halt in the shadow of one of the banks, or to make an adjustment in the path they were taking. Running while bent over made breathing difficult and sapped Allie's endurance. As if sensing his near exhaustion, Iskandar drew him up in the lee of a bend in the wash and made him sit down while she scanned the skies for the *thorga*.

"I believe it is seeking other prey," she said at last.

Like Allie, her chest heaved as she fought to catch her breath. Like him, she was perspiring—something he recalled the Alassals did not do. Grains of sand clung to her skin and to his. She squatted down beside him and offered him water. He drank sparingly to conserve it.

"How much further to the hills and the forest?" he asked.

Iskandar rose to look. Like the Alassals, she measured time as sleep and awake, and distance in measurements that did not correlate to anything familiar to him. "We will sleep once more before we arrive," she told him, and dropped back down.

"Do we have enough water?"

"There are trees and a stream where we will stop for sleep," she said.

Allie grimaced. "Sleep" could mean six to eight more hours of travel. He began to wish he had gotten himself into better shape. Iskandar, though winded, seemed to be in far better condition—something perhaps innate to her species. With that last word, he began to consider how life Below would be classified. Linnaeus would have the proverbial field day.

"You are troubled," Iskandar said.

He knew she was not referring to his fear of the *thorga*. "If that is how I appear, I apologize," he replied. "It is that I am a stranger in this land."

"That is not so. You are my friend, are you not? As I am yours. How can you be a stranger to me? Yes, it is so that you are not accustomed to this land, as you call it, but I am here with you. You have drunk my water. Protection includes teaching you that you, as well as I, belong to the land."

Allie exhaled her name and found a smile. With her statement, he found himself torn between staying in this land for the rest of his life, or—if it proved possible—going back Above. As he completed that thought, he realized he had not referred to Above as home. But what did that mean? What could it mean?

And what did it mean for Iskandar's stated desire for him to take her Above with him if he should find a way up? Did he want to ask her that now?

"You are still troubled," she said. Her hand on his thigh warmed him through the fabric of his trousers. "May I read you?"

The woegong chose that moment to emerge from Iskandar's pouch. It slithered across her legs and onto Allie's arm, which it ascended so it was face to face with him. Its head drew closer, until it touched Allie's cheek and incipient beard. It began a slow rubbing with its own cheek against his.

"Yes," Allie answered her. His voice sounded remote, and in mild shock. "If you wish."

He did not feel her enter his mind, nor did he know why he had given her permission to do so. All the while, the woegong caressed his cheek, and emitted a low sound he interpreted as purring. To secure itself, the creature had coiled around Allie's arm. Its fur was bristly, yet it did not irritate his skin.

"Oh," Iskandar said, but without inflection in her tone. "I understand."

He did not feel her withdraw. "Tell me."

She hesitated. "I see there are some matters and some questions you should resolve for yourself," she said slowly, thinking her way. "But you wish to know why I asked you to take me with you if you should find a way to Above. I am not myself certain that I know the answer to that. There is curiosity, of course, and the satisfying of it, but...there is more. I wish to be...I choose to be with you, my friend. You are on a course of discovery. Were I to be taken Above, I would find myself on that same course. I would then hope you would choose to be with me."

"As...as mates? As mated?"

Her purple eyes seemed to penetrate his. "Are you asking me?"

"I—I do not know the rules," he hedged. Nor did he know his own mind on the matter. Uncomfortable, he got to his feet. "I think we had better move on. We have," and now he laughed, "miles to go before we sleep."

The woegong returned to Iskandar's pouch.

~ * ~

Out of the wash, they made better progress. The land became less rugged, although in turn it grew steeper, to what Allie estimated was a five-percent grade. But there was lower land far off to his left, covered with a silver lid. It took him almost a minute to recognize the silver was the result of the reflection of the overhead light on water. What he was looking at was a great inland sea.

"That," he said, pointing with a shaky finger.

Iskandar glanced in the indicated direction but did not slow her pace. "It is the Narnot Shanz," she said curtly. "It does not concern us."

He repeated the term, adding a question mark.

Reluctantly she answered him. "It is a large body of water, as you would say. A narnot."

"I would say it is a sea, perhaps the bay of an ocean. And the Shanz? What is that, its reflection?"

Now Iskandar was even more hesitant. The tip of her tongue flicked over her lips, as if they were dry. "They are...the strongest of the moieties with borders on the edge of the narnot...of your sea, Allie."

He squinted in that direction. "I think those are, are boats of some kind."

"The netting and smoking of *yohagh* is one of the activities along the shore." She touched his arm. "Forgive me, you don't know. The *yohagh* is...similar to your fish, I think. They are quite good. We Lannar trade with them. You have seen our brick and our wood. The

Shanz have little access to their own resources."

"Construction materials," Allie said.

She had to think about that. He could almost feel her dredging up the words from some television program. "Yes, I believe so," she said at last.

"We should visit them."

She turned and stopped his progress with a rigid arm. Her eyes were now the color of lilac, and dulled by tension, perhaps by fear. "That is what we should not do, Allie."

"I do not understand."

"And I hope you never find the full meaning of understanding it. Allie…the work done around the narnot is…is not done voluntarily."

He blinked. "Are you talking about slave labor?"

This time she did not have to search her television experience for the word. "Yes." She tilted her head at him. "You see, Below is not so idyllic as you might imagine. Is this not so?"

"As Above, so Below."

She resumed walking. "From what I have seen on television, yes, I fear as much."

"You were reading me just then, Iskandar."

"I was, yes. I am sorry. I know you dislike this. But those of us in those moieties who are literate…is this word not correct? To be able to read?"

Allie had to laugh. "This sort of reading stretches the definition a bit," he conceded.

"The Lannar, and the Alassal, are open always," she said. "As are others. But the one who has a secret is one to be avoided."

"I think that may be true Above as well." His gaze took in the hills and mountains ahead. "I can almost make out some of the trees now," he said. "Where are we to sleep?"

"Sleep," she murmured.

Allie thought if Iskandar were human, her faint smile would be regarded as shy.

She pointed at a stretch of low hills a little to the right of their direction of travel. "You can see how your trees grow in rows along the banks of the stream. That is where we are going. And the gap into which we will go after we sleep has become more distinct. You can see where your tree has fallen into the water."

"You keep calling them 'your trees,'" he said.

"Yes. What you call a tree. Is this not so?"

"What do you call them?"

Iskandar considered for a moment. "*Sevvyl* is our word, and the Alassal word. There are of course others. We also have names for different kinds of trees." She gave him a sidelong look of curiosity as she strode next to him. "Do you wish to learn to speak Lannar?"

"No, but this raises an interesting question. I should have thought of it earlier. You are able to receive transmissions from Above. Are you able to transmit to Above as well?"

She did not respond at once. Instead, a look of dismay came over her face, as if she had just been asked the one question she was dreading. Finally she gave a little nod. "There is a control room at the base of the dish antenna. There, with some adjustments, it would be possible to transmit. But this will not happen, Allie. It cannot be allowed to happen."

A surge of hope had begun to fill him with her first words, but by the time she finished speaking, he felt empty. "But why, Iskandar?"

"Above does not know of Below," she replied, stepping around a clump of low shrubbery. They had reached a point where different vegetation thrived, dense enough to compel them to thread their way through it. "It is not to be informed of us. Even the Oiskin and the Degg and the Shanz understand this, in their own way. If our existence were to become...step around that, Allie!"

He did so. "What was it?"

"Our word is *igbonnu*. To you that means 'fire bush.' Note the leaves. They are covered with tiny venomous stingers." She took a few more steps in silence, before picking up where she had left off. "If we were to become known to the humans Above, they would spare no expense in finding a way down here. Already an attempt was made to learn what existed at this depth. But it did not reach...I should explain. There is more than one Below. We know of one because it is connected to us by what was at one time long ago a magma tube. Some moieties conduct trade through it. This other Below is connected to still others. Is this clear to you?"

"Yes, I understand, but I still don't see—"

"A shaft was dug that came very close to reaching Below. It was reported that those who dug it were able to hear voices."

"You're talking about the Kola Superdeep in northwest Russia," Allie said.

She shook her head. "I do not know what that is. What is said is the digging was stopped due to lack of funds." She glanced at him. "Funds are a form of money, are they not?" At his nod, she continued. "It is said the unreported reason was the voices. The diggers attributed them to ghosts and refused to continue. What they heard, of course, were the voices of another moiety in another Below, inside their heads."

"That hole goes down more than twelve kilometers," Allie said. Confusion made Iskandar blink. "Think of it as twelve thousand of these steps you and I are taking."

"Yes, thank you, but that is not important. Allie, we were almost discovered, by a species with a terrible record of exploiting and abusing people unlike themselves. We cannot, will not, allow that to happen to us." Struggling with herself, she found more words. "Allie, this is why I am myself torn with you. Yes, I wish to see Above. But I know in here," she touched her stomach, "in here that this must not happen. I wish to know, and I wish to avoid knowing, do you understand?"

Allie sighed. "Yeah. Yeah, I do, Iskandar. But tell me this: if I should find a way back to Above, would I be allowed to go?"

She looked away. Sadness crept into her voice, which shook as she answered him. "I—I do not know for certain. I think…I think I would fear for you, should you try."

"Then this trek is a fool's errand," he mumbled. "Iskandar, I'm sorry you had to make this trek, too."

"But this is not so, Allie. You have drunk my water." She cocked her head at him. "Still do you not understand?"

He stopped and turned to her. "I guess I don't, Iskandar. Is this …did I misunderstand you about being mated? I did not think you were serious—"

"No, you did not, I—"

"…because you seemed to find it amusing, so I took it simply as banter."

"Banter?"

"You know, light humor between two people."

She reached out to grip his arm. "No, Allie, that is not…" Exasperated with herself, she sighed.

"If I misunderstood—"

Her hand moved to his mouth, covering it. "We are not far

from the trees where we will sleep," she told him. "Let us discuss this there."

012: My Cup of Tea

The top of the low hill Mollow had chosen for sleep was sheltered by leggy shrubs that hung over soft blades of blue grass with orange variegation. The shrubs were no protection whatsoever from the elements, but no dark clouds had formed anywhere under the vaulted crystal, and only a few white ones. Although Thadie was prepared and even eager to rest, it appeared to her Mollow wanted to talk first. Both sat comfortably, Thadie in tailor-fashion, the Alassal with scaly legs outstretched. Although she had assumed they would talk, silence continued to reign between them. Content not to break it, Thadie leaned back against a shrub and closed her eyes. Still her mind rambled. Mollow had mentioned being open to knowledge, but she had withheld an expansion of the statement with the excuse it was not her place to... Thadie's lips pressed together. To what? What was Mollow trying to avoid?

"There are some matters you must resolve on your own," Mollow said.

Thadie's eyes flew open. "Are you...you're reading me!"

"Not so. I see your expression change, and your eyelids flutter. I hear your respiration and your heartbeat."

"Then tell me what I need to resolve," she demanded. A moment later, she added, "Please."

"You are not where you were."

"I *know* that! Don't you think I know that?"

The Alassal paid no attention to the frustration in her tone. "I do not fully understand your negative feelings for Allie."

"He is white!"

"Yes, he is," Mollow agreed. "And I am brown, for the most part, and my skin is covered with scales. I am different from you, as he is different from you. Yet you show me no negativity. What has Allie done to you to deserve it?"

"He is white," Thadie muttered.

"So you have pointed out. Please tell me how that fact answers my question."

"You don't understand," Thadie said looking away.

"But, unlike you, I am trying to understand."

"All right," Thadie said sitting up straight. "All right! For centuries my people were oppressed and demeaned and insulted by whites because we were black, and therefore were thought to be backward and inferior. This treatment will not be forgotten."

"I had no idea Allie was so evil," Mollow mused, hushed.

"Oh, he's not at all, but…oh, damn you."

"Just so," the Alassal said softly. "You accuse him of seeing white. Yet it is you who sees white, when you should see a person, an entity, a being much like yourself, with worries, likes, concerns, feelings, thoughts, dreams…much like you, Thadie. That is how he sees you. That is how he sees me, and Ssakileh, and Iskandar. That is how he sees Gullaf and Otero and Beterr." She slowed her words to add emphasis. "It is how he sees."

Thadie's mouth worked, but no sound emerged. Stunned into silence, she lost all control of her protests, her arguments, and her beliefs. Licking her lips did not help her find words. Her ribs began to ache; she was holding her breath while she waited for something in her mind to coalesce. But nothing formed there.

"If he finds a way," Mollow said firmly. "He will come for you. This I know."

She bestowed upon this statement the tiniest of nods.

"Do you wish to eat now?" Mollow asked.

"I don't know what I wish," she whispered hoarsely. "I wish to cry. I wish not to be seen crying. I wish to go home. I wish to think. I do not know what to think. The Earth is solid, yet I see it is not. Allie is white, yet you say he is like me."

"That is not so, Thadie. You have it in reverse of what you think. Your words should have been thus: 'You say he is like me, yet Allie is white.' Do you see the difference?"

She nodded hesitantly. "You are saying I deny myself the possibility he is in fact like me."

"Your door is closed, that much is so."

"And I should open it?"

"If you can. The bolt is stuck, and the lock is rusted. It will take some work to open it. The first step is to find the desire to open it."

"You ask much, Mollow."

"Life asks much of everyone." Mollow lay back on the grass. "Sleep on it, my friend."

Thadie's jaw dropped. Then her eyes began to leak. She tried without success to recall the last time anyone had addressed her as friend. Regular slow breathing beside her said Mollow was already asleep, unavailable for further questions or comments. Nothing remained but for Thadie to wonder whether she herself would dream. In that regard, her wishes were unclear.

She stretched out on the grass; her mind drifted and prepared itself to shut down for a while. A memory flitted by, and another. A pleasant day in Johannesburg. Dashing from the water because of a shark sighting. A climb up Table Mountain. Dinner with the Alassals. But all these soon faded, to be replaced by a voice.

Mollow's voice. Whispering over and over again in the emptiness of her mind. How was that possible? Now, unable to block the penetration of another's thoughts, she was compelled to listen.

"You do not treat people kindly with the expectation they will reciprocate. You treat people kindly because you yourself are kind."

At some point during the refrains, Thadie Mayane fell into a deeper sleep.

~ * ~

"I am solitary," Iskandar began.

They were sitting side by side on an outcrop of basalt that ran through the trees. Here the air was thick with moisture from the leaves and reminded Allie of stepping out of the shower stall after turning off the hot water. Yet the air was also mild around them. Having traveled far already, he was ready to lean against the tree behind him and doze off. But Iskandar had words for him.

"Because I am solitary, I am free to give my water to whomever I wish," Iskandar continued. "This entitles another to my protection and my comfort, if needed, if desired. This much I have told you."

"But there is more," Allie said, sensing a picture about to enlarge.

"There is more. If I am mated, and we should receive a visitor who drinks our water, we owe him or her protection if needed, that much remains true. But comfort is..."

"Exclusive?" Allie suggested.

"I do not know this word."

"It means you and he will mate—"

"Or she."

Astonished, he recovered quickly. "Yes, of course. The two of you will mate with no one else."

"That is exclusive?"

"In this sense, yes."

Iskandar considered this. "I shall share this word. Allie…I knew you were concerned about possible misinterpretations of the ways here Below. To put you at ease, I made light of that concern with regard to mating. Yet, because I remain solitary, and you have drunk my water, you may call upon me for protection and comfort. This is not lightly given, Allie. I have had visitors to whom I did not give water. Nor, outside of the rules for a visitor, do I lightly give comfort."

Allie frowned. "So you comfort me because that is one of the rules you live by."

Her jaw dropped a little, as if she had just recognized another interpretation of what she had told him. Her face took on a look of intense emotion, directed inward. "Oh, Allie…yes, comfort by Lannar rules, yes, but…but…when we took comfort together, you pressed your mouth against mine in a way I have seen on your television. This is a sign of like, is it not?"

"Of affection, yes, it can—"

Her mouth impacted on his as she threw her arms around him. She seemed not to know precisely what to do with her lips except press them against his, and he was too startled to attempt a lesson. He managed to break contact, although he was unable to extract himself from her embrace. Sensing something amiss, Iskandar herself pulled away.

"Did I do wrong?" she worried. "Was this wrong?"

He smothered a smile. "Well…no, but…" Nibbling an incisor at his lower lip failed to aid his thinking. "Iskandar…tell me if I'm wrong, but when you use the word 'mate,' it has more than one meaning. There is 'mate' to produce offspring, and 'mate' to engage in a relationship based on mutual affection." He finished by borrowing one of her pet questions. "Is this not so?"

"It is so."

Now he hesitated, for he was uncertain whether he wanted to know which meaning she meant to convey. Yet even that was incomplete, for she might have had both meanings in mind. Ssakileh had already told him reproduction was possible with a DNA splice.

Abruptly Iskandar looked away, only to dart a furtive glance back at him.

"What is it?" he asked.

"I am sorry."

"You were reading me."

"Because I affectioned you, and I sought to know how you feel. And I was not able to find an answer, because you yourself do not know."

He grimaced as one in anguish. Only partly did he know his own mind. "I wish to go home," he said. "I would take you with me, as I promised. But you tell me I cannot do either. But I wish to know for certain I cannot. I want to see the grave of Abner Perry."

Her face now showed no trace of emotion, but her voice was leaden. "Yes, of course. Sleep now, and we will continue our trek."

"Iskandar…"

But already she had turned away from him.

~ * ~

"Shh!" Mollow said, into Thadie's ear, waking her.

The urgency of the sound brought Thadie fully alert. What had happened? Another cave-in at the mine? Was anyone hurt? Killed? Blinking, she took in Mollow for the first time. "You're hurt!" she cried, and Mollow shook her, none too gently.

"You're dreaming. You were dreaming. Shh."

Thadie caught her breath. Gradually her heart rate subsided. She brought herself back to the present moment. She and the Alassal named Mollow were on a journey to find Allie. She recalled the collapsed floor in the Mandela Mine, and the terrifying ride down the slope, and waking in the Alassal moiety. "What's wrong?" she asked, hoarsely, for her throat was dry.

"There is a *thorga* hovering. It is best not to move."

Mollow, who had called her "friend," came into focus. She would explain the danger from the *thorga* when it was time. Thadie held still.

Mollow gave her the tiniest nod of approval, then turned her gaze through the overhanging shrubbery to the sky. Thadie looked as well. High above, like a hawk seeking prey, flew a winged creature much too large to be a bird. She thought it dwarfed even the condors she had seen in nature films. It seemed to be a variety of white, difficult to distinguish from the crystal vault above it.

"So that prey below cannot see it," Mollow said.

"You...you're reading me again?"

"You are my friend. To protect you, I must know what you fear."

Chuckling, she made a languid gesture. "That," she replied. "I fear that. But you are here."

"It is flying off. Keep still." As the creature grew smaller with distance, Mollow went on, "Thadie, I am here because you are my friend. But I do not understand how I could possibly be your friend. After all, I am Alassal, and you are human—"

"Oh, that doesn't matter..." And Thadie stopped, aghast. "*God in die hemel,*" she breathed. "You...you did that on purpose!"

"That is so."

Notions and visions raced through her mind. Words she had said, thoughts she had had, fears that had shaken her. Actions she had taken. Worst of all, things she might have done differently... done better.

"Perhaps it is that each of us is entitled to moments of perfect clarity," Mollow said, her voice so soft Thadie wondered whether it came as sound or telepathic.

She sat bolt upright. "We have to find him," she gasped. "I have to tell him." She scrambled to her feet, and tried to hoist Mollow to hers, without much success. "Come on," she pleaded. "*Kom saam met mi! Hamba nami!*"

The mix of Afrikaans and Zulu was too much for Mollow. "I do not watch so much television," she complained, finally rising. "Please, let us hold to your English."

But Thadie paused and brushed a splash of lilac petals from her hair. "Mollow," she said tenderly. "You *are* my friend."

"This I know," Mollow whispered.

"I have much to unlearn. It may take some time."

"We have that time." She looked out at the distant blue mountains. "We also have one more sleep before we arrive."

Thadie finally smiled. "I can take a hint. As you may have noticed."

~ * ~

Allie awoke to find himself alongside Iskandar, his left arm draped over her waist. As unobtrusively as he could manage, he withdrew the offending limb, fearful of what she might think if she should awaken. Separation accomplished, he rolled onto his back on the grass and peered up at the branches of the tall trees. Tree analogs, he reminded himself. Just as...

He blinked at the sudden thought. Just as the Lannar and Alassal and Oiskin and probably Degg were human analogs. Humalogs? He barked a laugh at that, and at the sharp sound Iskandar came directly awake, as did the woegong in her pouch, both scanning for predators.

"Sorry," Allie said, hanging his head. "It's all right. I was just... just..."

The woegong pulled itself back into the pouch. Iskandar dampened her alert state. "Why did you move your arm?" she asked.

"You are upset with me," he replied, mildly surprised by her awareness of him. "I did not want you to think I-I had taken a liberty."

"A what?"

"Touching you, when you sought no touch."

"But I am not upset. Allie, I wish to know how you feel, that is all."

"About what?" he blurted, belatedly realizing he already knew what.

"About me, Allie. Toward me. About us. I cannot find a reading."

His face twisted as one in pain. "Iskandar, how can you want us to be mated?"

"Did we not push our lips together in your fashion? Did I not wrap around you and take you inside me in my fashion? But those are actions. I wish to be mated with you, not for those matters...*not only* for those matters, but because we are very alike, you and I. You are curious, as am I. You are kind, as I hope I am."

"You are," he said. "More than kind."

"You seek adventure, as do I. There are matters of which I can teach you. There are matters of which you can teach me. In this way we can become more than we are. We are friends, are we not? We are companions on a common journey, is this not so? We like being together, do we not? At least, I like being with you, whether beside you or in comfort." Her face contorted as she looked away, and her voice filled with sorrow. "But I cannot read how *you* feel. I do not know what *you* think about these matters."

In that moment Allie knew he had found perfect clarity. All he needed now was the words with which to express it. On that effort, he feared he fell lame. "Iskandar...I think...to borrow a line from a song I heard in a movie...I think you are quite my cup of tea."

"Tea," she repeated dully. "A...a beverage, am I?"

He touched his lips to her forehead. "One I would drink to the very last drop."

013: New Dangers

Although Thadie's mood improved, the terrain did not. An escarpment barred their way not long after she and Mollow left their sleep site. For a few minutes they walked along it, looking for a way up and over. At last they found a spot where the lip of the escarpment had collapsed to form a climbable slope of loose detritus. The footing nevertheless was treacherous, and only by dint of hard effort did the two of them reach the crest and the grassland that lay beyond.

The glistening cream-white boulder half-buried in the ground several paces away caught their attention. It could be skirted readily enough, but it was obviously an outlier, and not a part of the geology of this area. Both females approached it cautiously. It seemed to be glowing from an internal source of power. A tentative touch by Thadie showed the boulder was no warmer or cooler than the air or the ground beneath it.

Thadie, who had taken a minor in geology from the University of Zululand, thought she recognized the mineral, and conducted a simple test to eliminate one possibility. Using a bit of copper jewelry from Mollow, she tried to scratch the crystal; it remained unmarked. "Not calcite, but quartz," she declared, returning the amulet. "Not a crystal, but in massive form." She looked around at the bare patches of rock and dirt exposed amid clumps of grass and low shrubs. "I don't understand. How did this get here?"

Mollow stared at the boulder for a while, then slowly lifted her face to gaze up to the overhead vault of light. After a moment, Thadie followed her yes.

"Oh, shit," she said softly.

"I have heard this sometimes happens," Mollow said. "But this is the first time I have seen one of these."

"Are we in danger?" Thadie asked, still looking up.

"This happens but rarely." Mollow looked at the range of hills and mountains on the horizon. "We should continue our journey."

From time-to-time Thadie glanced up as they continued on their way. Here in Below, the sky truly could fall. She wondered what caused it. Perhaps the weight of the boulder, applied over time, had eventually caused the crystal to fracture, and to separate along that fracture from the overall mass. But that explanation was incomplete. It was an effect of some force, not the cause of an event. Allie, whose avocation was geology, might know, but he was not here.

A gust of wind blew up, carrying with it dust not been held in place by vegetation. As it passed them, Thadie closed her eyes and mouth, and pinched her nostrils shut. Already she had learned that Below, all meteorological hints portended events. She wondered what was coming.

"It is a storm," Mollow said, reading her again. "One which you have not seen. The air swirls above us. Sometimes it drops down to the surface."

"You mean, like a tornado."

Mollow hissed agreement. "I have seen these on your television. But ours do not appear so strong as yours."

Madly Thadie whirled, looking around. She saw nothing imminent, and only two small gray clouds far away. "What can we do?"

"Much depends on its direction when it drops down. But it will not last for long. And it may not drop down at all." Mollow's gaze passed over the terrain to the foothills and the two gaps between the trees. "It will have formed long before we can reach them. We need to find…"

"What? What?"

Mollow's arm shot out, pointing. "There. We may find safety there."

Looking, Thadie saw only great blocks of stone, scattered on the terrain. They appeared to be a couple miles away. With a run of twelve to fifteen minutes, she and Mollow could reach them.

"What is that?" she asked Mollow, as they headed off in that direction. At first they walked fast, then broke into a jog. "It looks like it is still out in the open."

"There are mines in the quarry," Mollow said. "We will be safe there." She glanced back, and added, "If we can reach them in time."

Thadie cried out as she looked over her shoulder. Already, some five miles away, darker clouds had formed. But they seemed to be hanging high in the air, as if they were waiting for a signal to start.

"How long?" Thadie gasped.

"I cannot say. Perhaps we shall have time."

"*Perhaps?*"

"Is this word not correct?"

Thadie exhaled loudly. "Just run, Mollow. Just run."

~ * ~

"She does not have a name," Iskandar said, when Allie asked. "Do you wish to give her one?"

The grade of the terrain had reached six or seven percent, but appeared to grow no steeper. There was still one more sleep to be taken, at the grove still indistinct in the distance. Before that, the slope crested, and there was a downhill trek to the grove. Still, despite the slight incline here, the ground was unbroken and relatively easy to traverse.

Beside him, matching him stride for stride, Iskandar cast side-long glances now and then, but kept her counsel. Allie found it was easier to ponder than to breathe, even though he knew she was reading him. Openness was the way of things Below. It made secrecy —not impossible, perhaps, but certainly very difficult. It also required open diplomacy and commerce. Here there could be no warlike intents, for such would be read immediately. War was as futile as...

...as an attempt by him to make a baby with Iskandar.

The thought shook Allie. He wondered why that comparison had occurred to him. Inevitably the wondering led to a question of what the offspring would look like. The way Iskandar had described the process, the equivalent of a tadpole formed first, grew legs, probably lost a tail, and eventually emerged onto the land. A smile briefly lit his face as he recalled his grandfather had tenderly called him Tadpole when he was but a boy.

From war to tadpole, he told himself. Stream of consciousness.

They began to thread their way among clumps of flowering shrubbery. Great clots of turquoise petals rained onto the ground as they passed. Iskandar paused momentarily to collect a handful of them, offering a few to Allie and to the woegong, who had just poked its head from her pouch.

Munching on the petals, Allie wished he had not seen the woegong emerge. It reminded him of the radically different physiology of Iskandar. Surely no DNA splice could overcome that. Not that being unable to have a family was a deal-breaker, but...but...

Allie sighed and dismissed the question. Iskandar was enough, and more than enough. That notion led him to consider the future.

Finding a way out did not mean taking it. Even if he were not permitted, he could find a way to leave, and to take Iskandar with him. But then what? Above, no DNA splice would be able to let them reproduce. Only here, Below, was that at least theoretically possible. Again he was back to a family, and again he had to dismiss the idea.

"A name," he said, returning to Iskandar's question. "That depends. Is she going to remain with us?"

"They are affectionate. And loyal, once they take to someone."

Names escaped him. In the past, he had cared for several pets, mostly dogs, a couple of cats. What was a suitable name for a furry snake?

And he thought: why does it need a suitable name?

"Magenta," he said. "Maggie for short."

Iskandar hissed approval. "All right. But why?"

"You're not reading me?"

For a moment she was silent. Again she hissed her approval and nodded briskly. "She and I are much the same color. The one reminds you of the other, and it is a pleasant reminder. Thank you, Allie."

"In fact, to my eyes you are more violet. But that name does not lend itself to a short name."

"How would you shorten mine?" she asked.

Allie shrugged. "Sandy, perhaps, or Candy. But I happen to prefer Iskandar."

She responded with a litotes. "I am somewhat accustomed to it, myself."

It was a moment when he might have kissed her, but Magenta had an avid interest in the firlin pouch.

They continued across the terrain, each with thoughts, though Iskandar's were private, as he was unable to read her. Presently he noticed that, for some reason, it was a little darker Below. And creeping into hearing range there was a low sound unlike anything he had heard before. He turned around and looked up.

"Iskandar!"

Quickly she drew him along by the arm; he felt as if it were about to leave the socket. Wind began to whip them.

"I was not watching!" Iskandar cried out. "I should have been watching! Allie..."

Another glance back let him witness the birth of what he thought of as a dust devil. It was the color of the dirt in which the groundcover grew, a brownish sort of black, but mottled. In the context of the wind, it looked ominous. It was impossible to gauge its direction of travel, which shifted drunkenly. Rain began to pelt them, driven by the air current. The natural light from above grew darker still as the black clouds began to sweep over them. Off to their right formed another dust devil. As they ran, Iskandar bumped him to the left. They soon came upon a shallow ravine; rainwater had already gathered on the sand below. The wind became a fury, the dust particles now scouring them. Without warning, Iskandar shoved him into the ravine. He landed on his butt and back, and air burst from his lungs with the impact. He looked up at Iskandar, now standing at the top of the bank. Her hand dipped into the pouch, grabbed Magenta, and threw her down. Swept by the wind, the woegong landed on his stomach. He held out his arms to Iskandar. She bent her knees and was about to jump down when a dust devil scooped her up into the air.

"Allie!" she screamed disappearing into the whirling cloud.

014: Resolutions

The sprint for the stones left Thadie holding her sides and fighting to catch her breath. But she could not stop yet; Mollow would not allow it. The Alassal dragged her down into the quarry itself. Around them, bits of debris began to fly. Some pelted her—fragments of twigs, and tiny pebbles. Just ahead she spied an opening, a mineshaft. The support frame at the entrance appeared ready to give way. But there was no other choice of refuge. Mollow made for it, tugging at her urgently. Thadie found just enough of a second wind to stagger along beside her. The air around them filled with shrieks as the howling wind passed over the stones. Something solid, an uprooted tree perhaps, struck one of the stones; she heard the fracturing of wood. She dared not look. Only the mineshaft opening mattered. That, and the friend who was pulling her along, to save her.

Three running paces, two, and they were in darkness, illuminated only by whatever light managed to filter into the mine from above. Still they did not stop moving. Mollow yanked her deeper into the shaft. The territory was all too familiar to Thadie, but she took no solace from that fact. A furious wind howled past the entrance. An uprooted tree slammed into it. And the supports finally gave way, leaving them in dust and utter darkness.

"I have a light," Mollow said, close beside her. "Close your eyes."

Thadie did so. A moment later she heard a scratching sound, and smelled smoke. Alarmed, she opened her eyes.

Mollow had lit a candle. She held it here and there to examine the interior of the shaft. A couple of the overhead supports showed signs of decay, but lines of wires along the walls led further into the shaft, though the electricity that powered them came from a generator long ago shut off. A series of small illuminative spheres, evenly placed, showed where light might be emitted. But the candle-light died in the darkness of the deeper regions. The end was too far away to see.

"There's no way out," Thadie said. The collapse at the entrance held no fear for her, even though rescue from without was unlikely. "There's no breeze. Do you feel?"

"It is so." She drifted back toward the entrance, slowly enough the candle did not blow out with the movement. "We might clear this rubble, but in doing so we might risk further collapse."

"It will not clear itself," Thadie said moving a small boulder out of the way. Before continuing, she straightened, watching Mollow affixe the candle to a narrow ledge on the wall. "Mollow, we have one other possibility. It entails no immediate risk, but I don't know if it will be successful."

"Another option is always welcome. What is yours?"

~ * ~

She knew, Allie thought. *Iskandar knew she might not make it.* He caressed the woegong, now coiled around his left arm. "She knew, Maggie," he whispered. "She saved you…she saved *us*."

Magenta chittered in response, in a language he would now never learn. Iskandar had saved them, and now she was gone. Her passing left his heart torn into many small pieces, and it was only the coil of fur around his arm that kept the pieces from flying apart.

A surge of hatred for Below welled into Allie and enveloped him. It filled him with a terrible resolve. He *would find* a way out, and regardless of what the Lannars or Alassals or Oiskins or *anyone* down here wanted, he was *leaving*. He was going back to Above. If anyone tried to stop him…if anyone killed him for trying to leave, he would welcome that release, for then and only then would he see her again. See Iskandar. Win-win.

Only now had he come to see he had fallen in love with her.

Magenta chittered.

Ignorant of the language, he chose his own interpretation. "Yeah. Yeah, I'll take you with me. We'll find some seedy apartment in the dregs of New York. You'll grow into a blimp on the roaches."

His blurred vision searched the horizon for the gap that led to the grave of Abner Perry. The answer was there. It *had to* be there. Because he could no longer abide remaining Below.

Something very soft brushed his cheek. Magenta was licking his tears away.

Onward Allie went, trudging at first, then picking up his feet. He aimed himself at the gap Iskandar had pointed out, where the grave of Abner Perry might—or might not—hold the key to going back to Above. Never losing sight of his goal, he picked his way around low shrubs, skirted uneven terrain in favor of unbroken. And all the while, Magenta remained coiled around his arm.

At a brook they paused for a brief rest and a drink of water. Magenta slipped down and, careful to avoid getting wet, took several laps with her rough tongue. Allie chose water from his canteen, water Iskandar had given him. The memory of that brought fresh tears to his face. He made fists, fighting to remain in control of his emotions. To succeed in his quest—as he regarded it now—he needed clarity of focus.

After he extended his arm so Magenta could return to her perch, a sharp pain like a lightning bolt struck his mind. Even Magenta chittered out a cry of agony and tightened her coils around his arm as he dropped to his knees, head in his hand as he rocked back and forth in agony. The pain ebbed, and in its place he imagined he heard a voice. The words were incomprehensible, but the gist was transparent. He looked off to his right; he was to head in that direction.

Recovering, he changed course. Magenta chittered wildly, as if with excitement. Allie felt the onset of a headache.

~ * ~

"I do not know," Mollow said. "I cannot tell. As far as I know, no one has even attempted to do this." She looked down with distaste at the rocks and the rubble. "We have to continue as if it did not work."

The dust made breathing difficult. Thadie spat, but her mouth was too dry to clear the dust from it. She had experienced this before—at one time or another, all miners did—but on those occasions there was someone hastening to the rescue. She picked up a fist-sized rock and started to toss it aside, as she had done to a hundred other rocks here. Instead, she recalibrated her throw and hurled the rock violently against the mineshaft wall, adding a curse in Zulu for good measure.

"It will be all right, my friend," Mollow said softly. "We will get out of here."

Thadie drew a deep breath despite the dust and coughed it back out. "The candle has only a few more minutes of light left," she replied. "Do you have another?"

Mollow rolled a large boulder away from the debris. "I do not," she said.

Thadie resumed climbing to the top of the rubble and cast down more rocks. After she had cleared several of them, still no light seeped into the shaft. The lack of success ground at her. Surely by now she should see some light. A larger rock, much longer than wide, was wedged between the shaft ceiling and a smaller boulder. Tugging furiously, she soon moved it into a position where she could wriggle it free and cause more debris to spill down to the bottom of the pile. When finally it released, she was deluged with gravel and tumbled down the slope.

Mollow helped Thadie to her feet, and helped dust her off. The candle flickered but held on for the moment. Dust particles obstructed some of the light. The faces of Mollow and Thadie were cast in shadow. The light was so dim colors failed to register in their eyes. Only their silhouettes, dark against dark, revealed their presence.

The candle died, and with it, hope. Silence now reigned, broken only by the infrequent spill of dust and dirt, and coughing spells.

Presently Mollow spoke, her throat dry. "Perhaps I was too strong," she said. "I should try your idea again."

"What good would it do?

"What harm can it do?"

Thadie sighed. "You're right. We take whatever measures we can, until we no longer can. When you've finished, come join me, and let's move some more rocks."

In the dark she trod carefully to the pile, nudging it with her toe to ascertain its base. With equal care she climbed to the top and began again to send down a hail of rubble.

"I think I have," Mollow called out. "I do not know."

"Have what?"

"Not words, but a beacon of sorts. I just do not know…I am sorry, Thadie."

"I could use a couple more—" She screamed as a ray of light shot along the shaft to fade in the distance.

A rock moved; now another moved as well. Thadie, in stunned disbelief, watched a hand reach in over the top of the debris and pat the rocks as if feeling for something. She grasped it, clutched it, refused to release it.

"I'm not done with that hand yet," Allie said.

~ * ~

The excavation, from both sides, took a little over an hour. When the opening was large enough for Mollow and Thadie to fit through, they clambered outside and spilled down the slope. Allie tried to ease their descent, but was unable to steady both of them, with the result no one was steady, including himself. The three wound up in a tangle at the base of the debris, bruised and shaken. Mollow and Thadie blinked in the light from above, while the three liberated themselves from each other.

Allie took a seat on a boulder, hunched over, coughing and retching. Thadie brought him a bottle of water from Mollow's pouch and sat down beside him. Passing the bottle to him, she touched his hand inadvertently, but did not withdraw. Allie twisted on the rock to face her, a smile finding a way through his dusty, dirty, sweaty face. For several long seconds he looked down at the sepia hand on his dirty white.

"Thadie?" he whispered—all he could manage at the moment. He took a sip from the bottle and rinsed his mouth, then spat and took several more sips.

"Much has changed in me," she told him, and looked around. "Where is Iskandar?"

A burst of tears left tracks on his dirty cheeks. He looked away and swallowed hard. "Storm…" he said tightly. "Storm…took her. She's…gone."

"Oh, I am so sorry," Thadie gasped, reaching out to embrace him, to console him.

Allie withdrew immediately. "Thadie, what…?"

She sat back, regarding him with unflinching eyes. "Much has happened," she said again. "We may talk later. For now…I can only say I have found a friend." She placed a gentle emphasis on the last word.

He glanced at Mollow and spoke her name.

"Just so," she replied, and tilted her head as she looked at him. "I hope I have found another."

He grasped her hand and gave it a tight squeeze. "I never saw it any other way, Thadie."

For a long time they were quiet. Mollow joined them, seating herself on the dirt and gravel. Together they emptied the bottle of water. Allie rubbed his head as if it still ached. Magenta completed her search for grubs among the rocks and took up her place on Allie's arm...somewhat to Thadie's consternation. Allie's brief introduction and explanation quelled her agitation.

"Now what?" Thadie finally asked, very quietly.

"We find Abner Perry's grave," Allie answered immediately. His tone harbored no doubt or hesitation. "Now, more than ever, I want to get out of here."

"I...all right, Allie."

"Isn't that what you want?" he asked.

"I...wish I knew for certain. I understand some things now about...about myself. And Gullaf said there is mining work..."

"I can't stay here, Thadie. Not after..."

"I understand."

He looked out at the terrain and pointed. "You can just see it," he said. "That's where we're headed. A grove of trees by a creek. Two hours, I think. Maybe three. We were g-going to s-sleep..." He shook his head, unable to continue.

"You fell in love with her," Thadie said, astonished.

"I fell in love with her," he said. "And I d-didn't get to t-tell her."

Abruptly he stood up and held out his hand to them. In his expression, determination mixed with grief. "A couple more hours, and then we can rest."

015: Getting to Know Oneself

The way was longer than it appeared. It seemed to Allie the grove was receding with each step they took toward it, as if it were teasing them. At times the air above the trees seemed to shimmer, a mirage above the savannah. Between him and the grove were black spots, some of which appeared to be moving. He wondered whether all this could be attributed to his headache, which was slowly worsening as the moments passed.

A dark brown hand on his arm got his attention. He glanced sharply at Thadie; she was not comporting herself as he had come to expect. She claimed a change but had yet to explain it. Her eyes looked worried.

"It's okay to grieve," she said, very softly.

His response came bitter as vetch. "Thanks. I was trying not to think about...it."

"I've known people in this situation before," she said, still quietly. "In the mines, things happen. Please believe me, it's easier to get past it if you face it. If you acknowledge your sadness, your...loss."

Allie fought to maintain his composure. "Thadie, I know what you're trying to do, and I'd like you to stop it." Then he lost it and whirled on her. "*What is it* with you, anyway?" he almost shouted. "You hate me, and then you want to be friends? Is it about me touching you when I kept you from falling? Is it...it...oh, *argh*. Just leave me alone."

He turned and continued walking, but not before he saw her glance at Mollow, who shook her head. He strode faster now, not quite fleeing, not quite holding back.

"I never hated you," Thadie said, catching him up and struggling to stay alongside him. "I just didn't...understand myself. Some things about myself. But this is no time for me to enumerate my laments, Allie. Believe it or not, I'm worrying about you."

"Then stop worrying."

She sighed. "That's not what friends do."

"We're not friends."

"Only from your point of view."

Again he stopped and turned to her. "You certainly are determined."

"About like I was when I kept you from falling over the front of that rock we were sliding on."

That stung him. "Yeah, you did that."

"And that was when you thought I hated you. Which I don't, but…well, there it is. Allie, I'm more me now. I'm closer to the person I am supposed to be. I've some distance yet to go. And I am trying so hard not to make this about me. I'm not important. This is about you. It's about seeing you through this, somehow. You've lost someone you love; that never stops hurting. I've seen it often enough. But life—"

"If you tell me that life goes on, I will…" He bunched a fist but pounded it against his own hip.

"I'll do even worse, then," she whispered. "I'll ask you what she would want of you."

He stood still and silent, while she watched over him. For a time, his mind emptied. The question she had asked was a weapon against him, and he had no defense for it. What would Iskandar want? What would she say, or tell him to say? All he could see was the cloud engulfing her, wresting her away from him forever. But she would say…

A deep breath quieted his heart and eased some of the anguish. "You are important, Thadie," he said.

Her hand was on his arm again. "Allie…"

He was not ready to meet her eyes. "She saved us. She saved Magenta and me. She thought of us first. And it was too late to escape the…the tornado. The last thing she ever did was call out my name."

"Then she died a hero."

"Would that I had died with her. Or that she had lived."

Thadie did not respond. He wondered whether she was encouraging him by her silence, to allow him to reach his feelings on his own. She had that sort of experience at the mines. That realization startled him: where he was now, emotionally, she had been, at least second-hand. Unable to empathize, not having lost anyone herself, she still showed high compassion. As she was showing now.

He brushed tears from his face and was unable to stop the flow of them. Her arms slung around him. She held him. While he was quaking with grief, she held him.

He thought it was good to have a friend.

~ * ~

With Allie's mood somewhat improved, they set out again. The black dots remained and grew larger. Some time later, they resolved into some sort of cattle. There were perhaps fifty of them.

"*Deekabos*," Mollow said. "Herds are best avoided." She nudged him toward a path that would allow them to circle the herd, hopefully unnoticed.

"Will they charge?" Thadie asked.

Allie found himself unable to resist. "Probably pay cash." But laughter at his own quip quickly morphed to more tears, and Thadie and Mollow eased him through.

"At the sight of us, they could stampede. If they do, they will lose all sense of direction. There is a wash over to the right. If we cross that, we will be safe even from a stampede," Mollow said.

"That gets my vote," Allie said.

"Mine as well," Thadie said.

A moment later, that vote was confirmed by an unexpected event. Out of the very grass on which the *deekabos* were feeding arose a blue beast that Above might have been called a panther. Its coloration blended well with the surrounding grass. A *deekabos* calf bleated, the sound reaching Allie a good ten seconds later. By that time the calf was dead and the herd scattered.

Allie, who had watched Nature films, and Thadie, who lived where such scenes were filmed, could only stare at the tableau. Mollow nudged them both. "Perhaps a retreat is in order," she suggested. She led them away and into a more rugged terrain dotted with sparse clumps of shrubs, where there was better cover, and they were less likely to be noticed.

In an awed voice Thadie asked, "What *is* that?"

"Keep moving," was Mollow's only response.

They used the shrubbery for concealment as they walked over treacherous terrain. A misstep in one of the holes could wreck an ankle—Allie thought of the holes as kettles, formed when clots of glacial ice melted, but there was no visible evidence of glaciers ever having formed here. A spill into a shallow ravine might do worse damage. Allie glanced back...and gasped.

The herd had dispersed, most of the black spots now near the horizon. But of the great blue carnivore, nothing could be seen. Where had it gotten to? Wildly he looked around now. "Mollow, where…?"

"Down here," she ordered. "Into this ravine."

Allie and Thadie did not hesitate following her down the steep slope. Fortunately, there were ledges and small outcrops for footholds and hand holds. Allie followed Mollow so they could catch Thadie if she slipped. Once at the bottom, they could just peek over the tip of the bank, but there was little to see, for the vegetation that concealed them now blocked much of their view.

"Mollow?" Allie said again.

She rose up a little higher by altering her shape. After a long look, she dropped back down. "It is a *kkarreeg*," she told them. "In its natural state it resembles…an offspring of Allie and myself."

"Wait," Allie said. "You mean it can change its shape? It's a shapeshifter?"

"That is so. The *kkarreeg* becomes a predator, the better to hunt and kill. And keep your voice down."

"What does it eat?" Thadie asked.

Morrow was noncommittal. "Whatever it wants. But they hunt so their people may eat."

"People," Allie said heavily.

"Oh, yes, they are quite intelligent, and voracious. The *kkarreeg* developed the serum that protects all of us."

"Serum?" Allie asked. "What serum?"

Mollow continued to scan the savannah for signs of *kkarreeg*. Finally she seemed satisfied, and helped Allie and Thadie climb up from the ravine. As they began walking once more toward the grove where they would sleep, Mollow returned to Allie's question.

"I cannot say how long ago this was," she began. "Perhaps two hundred of your years. Gullaf might know. But there was a visitor from Above, and shortly after she arrived, Alassals began to sicken, and some died. An examination of their blood by those whose work included the ability to know, found what you would call bacteria or microbes in this blood. The effects were studied and generalized, so that one could develop a serum that would protect against any such attacks on anyone—Alassal, Lannar, Oiskin, Degg, Shanz…anyone. Including humans."

"I'm willing to be vaccinated," Allie said. Thadie nodded quick agreement.

Mollow looked at them in some surprise. "But you already have been made immune. Like us and all others in Below, you cannot now be made sick."

"Wait." Allie almost tripped on an exposed root. "What? *How?*"

"When you ate the *yagoah* at our first meal," she explained.

"That thing that tasted so bad, that I wasn't supposed to chew?" he exclaimed. "That was the serum?"

"It contained the serum, that is so. You need never concern yourselves with illness again, of any kind, Below or Above."

"But you should have given us a choice," Thadie put in. Sweating, she plucked her parchment garment from her skin. "Medical experiments have been performed on my people. We have learned the hard way not to tolerate this."

"We meant no harm, my friend."

Thadie made a sound of disgust. "That's what they all—"

"Yes, that is so," Mollow broke in. "That is what they all say. Thadie, I promise you, when the Alassal tell you no harm was meant, then no harm was meant."

"What happened to the dead?" Allie wanted to know.

"They were eaten."

Both Allie and Thadie gasped.

"Everything eats something," Mollow said. "The *thorga* and the *paxys*, and even the *kkarreeg* will eat carrion."

"Carrion!" Thadie sputtered.

"Nature always cleans up, if allowed to do so." She pointed. "There, over the next rise. We have almost arrived at the sleep grove."

"But don't you bury them, or cremate them?" Allie asked.

Mollow shot him a look that clearly said she was puzzled. "Why would we do that?"

"To-to respect the *dead*," Allie cried.

Mollow hissed understanding. "That is wasteful. You are speaking of retaining the memory of the dead, Allie. That is as it should be." She touched her head and her stomach in turn. "We remember the dead always. In doing so, we cherish the memory of them. This is what you do as well, is it not? The bodies are but the containers of who we truly are. Here," again she touched her head and her stomach, "and here. This is where we honor and cherish them."

Allie gnawed at the lining of his cheek. "I…cherish…Iskandar …," he breathed.

"That is so, Allie." Mollow's voice was barely audible, even in the quiet air. "As well do I. She was my friend, too."

Anguish filled his voice as he said, "Oh, Mollow. Yes, of course she was. I'm sorry."

Thadie touched Allie's arm. "I wish I had known her." Her face twisted with realization, but she kept her hand in place. Her next words were sour but directed at herself. "I think that may be the kindest thing I ever said to a white man."

Mollow hissed, but in a tone neither of them recognized. "Thadie, my friend, when you can say that may be the kindest thing you ever said to a man, your rusted bolt will be halfway drawn."

Thadie moved in front of Allie, to bring him to a stop. Hands on his chest now, she touched her forehead to his ragged shirt. "Truly I wish I had known her, Allie," she said, and slowly pulled away.

"We are almost there," Mollow announced, looking ahead.

"Yes," Thadie whispered. "I think so."

016: Damage Control

Before they reached the rise, however, there were obstacles in the form of a rugged, broken terrain riven by narrow washes. At least the land was not impassable, just difficult. Conversation at this point was minimal, breath needed more for effort and abrupt changes in direction. From time-to-time Mollow helped her charges to surmount obstacles—a steep slope up and down, a collapsed outcrop, a dense clump of shrubbery.

As they approached another shallow ravine, Allie realized Thadie was not with them and turned back around to locate her. He and Mollow spotted her almost hidden about fifty paces away, sitting on a boulder, with her left foot resting on her right knee. Allie called out to her.

Her response did not carry well to them. "It's all right," she said. "I have a couple of stones in my shoe. You go on, I'll catch you up." She gave them a desultory wave and resumed working the stones loose.

"We'll wait for you in the ravine," Allie said.

He and Mollow continued on. The sides of the ravine proved very steep, but on their side part of it had collapsed, making descent relatively easy. When they reached the sand bed at the bottom, Allie looked around and kicked at some detritus. "This wash hasn't flooded in quite a while," he concluded. "There's no sign of waterflow around these rocks." He bent down. "And this looks like…gold. It's a little gold nugget embedded in this chunk of quartz."

"Keep it," Mollow suggested. "We make wire filaments and form them into decorative or artistic designs." She peered over the top of the ravine. "I do not see Thadie…" she muttered.

Allie looked, too. "Where could she…?" His arm shot out, pointing. Alarm filled him. "There," he cried, and started to climb out of the ravine. "Who are those people?"

Mollow yanked him back. "Those are Deggs," she said quietly. "They have been known to capture strays while they are out hunting."

Allie counted seven of the Deggs. "We have to—" he began.

Again Mollow tugged at him. "There are too many of them for

us to fight. If I change to a defensive shape, they may well kill her before they flee. Such is their practice if they are endangered."

"But we have to do something!"

Mollow hissed frustration. "I know. But...but what?"

The Deggs were now almost half a mile away by Allie's reckoning. He pulled out the revolver Iskandar had given him. "But I have this," he said.

"A pistol. But unless you can kill all of them at once with it, someone will dispatch Thadie. No, Allie, that is not the way here. You are not on your television."

"That was uncalled for, Mollow," he groused.

"I was only trying to—"

He cut her off, unwilling to hear it. "Please," he snapped. "I'm trying to think here."

"We need help," Mollow said. "And it is far away."

"I know that. And Thadie is getting further away..."

A short silence intervened after his voice trailed off. "What is it?" Mollow pressed. "Have you an idea?"

Allie put away the revolver and gathered up his Swiss army knife. For a few moments he hefted it in his hand, still thinking hard. Gradually his countenance brightened, even as his heart pounded with worry.

"I see your plan," Mollow said, reading him. "It might work..."

"But can you do it?"

Mollow looked dubious. "I have never even considered it," she said. "I do not know what distance I would be able to traverse."

"Mollow, we have to try."

"She is my friend, too, Allie. Of course we have to try. I wish there were a better way."

He started to climb out of the ravine. "While we debate this, she is further away."

"Yes. Yes, of course."

~ * ~

At first, Thadie had shed tears—rage at having been trapped, fear of what might happen next. But the true danger lay in her destination. With a rope around her neck, and the other end tightly held by one of the group who had captured her, she was not about to escape, even though her hands were free. She was reminded, however, of the early slave trade practices, when others were dragged away in like manner to waiting ships. The thought sickened her. That it could be happening to her, here and now, terrified her.

Thadie glanced back. Already they had traveled far enough she was no longer able to see either Allie or Mollow. The chances of rescue from that quarter seemed remote. What could the two of them do against seven armed males. Did they even know she was missing? And who were these males? She did not understand a word they said. Their orders were punctuated sharply by fierce tugs at her rope. Come here, go there.

Clearly males, they wore no clothing and had very little hair on their pale blue skin, most of it in the form of coppery tufts on their heads, the backs of their hands, and along their spines. Their weapons included knives, hatchets, spears, and netting. Over the back of one of them was slung some sort of animal with mottled tan fur, possibly a youngling. Blood still trickled down the bearer's back.

Thadie managed to narrow down her fate to two options: as a captive, she would be enslaved, or made to be a mate, which really was the same thing; or she might be the main course at the next festival. She could see no other options. Neither alternative could be countenanced. Nor was escape an option, for how could she free herself and run fast enough? And in which direction?

Her capture had come so quickly. In one moment, she was refitting her shoe after clearing the stone from it. In the next, rough arms had clutched at her from behind, a hand covering her mouth before she could emit a scream. The noose came quickly and efficiently, as if the maneuver was one of long practice. Then the blow to the head...

Regaining consciousness, she found two males carrying her. When they saw her open eyes, they dropped her onto the hardpan and yanked her upright so that she might walk. At first she staggered helplessly, still fighting disorientation. She fell but once, to be dragged along the ground until she regained her feet and eventually her equilibrium. She resolved not to fall again, or to show any other signs of weakness.

As yet none of the males had made toward her what she thought of as advances. She considered her responses if one should occur. Not that she could defend herself physically, but the circumstances might arise in which she would be able to employ her favors to her advantage. Unfortunately, she had no experience at this, and in any event she had no idea what would motivate any of the males. Certainly, dressed in a now-ragged parchment shift, and stained by sweat and grit, she was hardly in a state of allure. She would have to consider other weapons, and ideas were not forthcoming.

If only Gullaf were here. He could transform into a T. rex and devour half the males at one bite. She fell into thoughts of him to help steady her emotionally. Yes, if he knew of her plight, he would come for her...somehow. Was she not an honorary member of the Alassal moiety? Had he not transformed for her and hinted at a coupling? That notion served to comfort her. Mollow was also of the Alassal, and surely she would come for her. And Allie...she did not know him well, but she considered him the kind of man who would come for her. But the terrain behind her was empty each time she glanced back.

The males were walking in single file now, with Thadie bringing up the rear. The terrain here, between two escarpments of dark red rock, was passable, but only just; it was not possible to walk two abreast. An idea came to Thadie that if she turned and ran, the males would be unable to conduct a mass pursuit of her until they were out of the *kloof*. She was a runner, and had participated, if unmedaled, in the Pan-African Games. Once in the open, she might not be recaptured. But the loop had been drawn taut around her neck, and the other end was now secured around the waist of the male who led her. She needed a cutting tool, and none was available...unless she could take the knife from the male's cincture, an action to be attempted only as a last resort.

Thadie had almost decided to make the attempt when they emerged from the narrow passage and spread out again. *She who hesitates*, Thadie thought, now angry with herself and her fears.

The hunting party had not taken more than a dozen paces from the *kloof* when a shadow passed over them. A shriek split the air above them. The males recognized the raptor's cry; so did Thadie. She looked up to see a great, dirty-white bird diving toward them. The males scattered back toward the cover of the *kloof*, dragging Thadie along with them. Terror drove her as well, as she recalled a *thorga* made even Mollow cautious. But the great bird reached the bottom of its stoop and struck the male who held her rope.

The sight that now greeted her eyes froze her in place. Impossibly, Allie leaned over to snag her rope. His legs were wrapped tightly around the neck of the *thorga*. Magenta was coiled around his arm. He wielded a little knife with a red handle and deftly sliced through the rope, liberating her…while she stood paralyzed in utter awe, her eyes huge and round.

"Come here!" he yelled, as the *thorga* prepared to lift off again. "Hurry, Thadie!"

Thadie unfroze and darted forward. From the *kloof* came cries of fear, accompanied by spears and hatchets thrown. Several struck the feathers of the great bird, but without apparent damage. Allie reached for her as she drew near and yanked her onto the *thorga*'s neck. The point of a spear missed her, but the haft struck Allie's head in passing, and he started to spill from the neck. "No!" Thadie screamed catching his arm and holding him in place. The *thorga* had to be Mollow. "Go!" she yelled. "Go, Mollow!"

"M'all right," Allie said, woozy. Her grip tightened on his arm as he tottered. Dazed by the blow, he collapsed against Thadie as the great bird took to the air.

Vertigo slammed Thadie as she looked down. She had no measure of the altitude; it might have been a few hundred meters. Mollow's wings seemed weaker and she soared rather than flapped. With her free hand Thadie liberated herself from the noose. Her expression now filled for the moment with loathing and disgust, she cast the rope away and watched it flutter down to the rocks well below. With the act, she recovered from her vertigo.

Allie's head lolled as he regained consciousness. He gazed up at Thadie with unfocused sepia eyes. "The face is familiar," he murmured.

"This was crazy," Thadie said. "You know that."

His words slurred. "Had to be done. Had to get you back."

She bent her head to kiss his forehead. "Thank you."

"That's what friends are for."

Tears began to well in her eyes. "Me," she said, chuckling. "Friends with a white man."

Allie gave her a pained look. "Not that again."

"No, no." She dried her eyes with the back of her hand, leaving a dirty smudge across her forehead. "Oh, no, Allie, I—I quite like it."

The *thorga*—Mollow—began to falter. Losing altitude fast now, she fought to hold her descent steady, in an effort to level out as they neared the ground. The left wing gave out altogether, and the body tilted in the other direction. Thadie screamed, almost spilling from the neck. Allie managed to grasp her arm. The ground was coming up too quickly.

"Mollow!" Allie cried, as the tip of the right wing caught against a boulder and a bone snapped audibly. The great body wheeled to the right and skidded over rocks, and finally came to a halt in a cloud of sand and dust. It transformed almost immediately to an unconscious and limp Mollow. Both Allie and Thadie spilled onto the ground as Mollow landed. They arose, bruised and bleeding, and rushed to the Alassal, with Allie checking on Magenta on the way. The woegong appeared bemused by all the activity and clung tightly to his arm.

Allie knelt beside Mollow and felt her throat for a pulse. There was none, but that meant nothing, for hers was a far different physiology.

"Is she?" Thadie fretted. "She's not, is she?"

"I can't tell. I don't think so."

Her right arm seemed to lie at an odd angle; fearing it was broken—it had been the wing that had scraped against the ground—he left it as it was. On her back, blue blood issued from a gash caused by one of the spears. There was more blood on her left hip, where a hatchet blade had struck it. He knew Mollow carried first-aid equipment in her pouch, but until she rolled over, the pouch was inaccessible, and he was reluctant to move her just yet.

Thadie pointed. "Look, there's the grove," she cried. "We're not even a hundred meters away."

"We can't leave her."

"Never," Thadie said. "You don't know it, but I was almost swept away in a flash flood. All that saved me was her grip on my arm. When I called out for her not to let me go, she replied, 'Never!' So I will not leave her, Allie."

He stood up. "We could carry her, but…I don't want to risk any bones she might have broken." He looked her over. "Are *you* all right?"

"I'm…shaken."

"But not stirred?"

Thadie flashed a grin. "You'll pay for that." Abruptly she sobered.

"Allie, when they took me, I was scared more than I thought I was. I tried to be strong, but I knew that was going to be impossible. All I had going for me was the hope that somehow Mollow and you...and you did."

"As I said, Thadie."

"Yes. What friends are for." Narrowed eyes regarded him. "Despite all this, I want to stay here, Below. I will have a better life here. I love mining work. I might not be a supervisor, not right away, but...but this is something I know. And Gullaf has been supportive. So: what about you? Will you stay?"

Sadly he shook his head. "I can't stay, not now. Not after..."

Mollow groaned, and immediately snagged their full attention. They knelt on either side of her. Allie supposed it was useless to ask her where it hurt, as there had to be numerous aches and pains. But he asked anyway, hoping she could hear him.

"Everywhere," Mollow answered, struggling to sit up.

"You're reading me again."

"I think my arm is broken."

"I'm sure it is," Allie said. "Anything else?"

"Just...sore."

Thadie stood up. "I'll be right back," she said. "And I'll need a little of your rope."

"It's in her pouch."

Allie sat back and inspected Mollow once again. The bleeding on her back and hip had already stopped, the blood coagulating to dull blue scabs. In sitting up, she had not seemed to favor any particular area, although she was careful not to use her right arm. He looked past her to the grove. It had been his and Iskandar's sleep destination. He wondered whether he would be able to sleep there, knowing that. Mollow's three-fingered left hand touched his thigh, and caressed him, before slipping back down to the ground. He decided to give up fretting over her reading of him.

Thadie returned with three stems of a shrub, broken off. Each was about half an inch in diameter and a yard long. Her job Above had to require emergency first-aid, and she undoubtedly knew a lot more than he about it. He passed her the Swiss knife and waited for instructions.

It was the right forearm that was broken. Gently Thadie ran her curved hand over it, feeling for the fracture, but not finding it. "I don't think we have to set it," she told Allie. She lifted the arm a little. "Does it feel as if it is grating?" she asked Mollow.

Mollow shook her head. "I know my body. It's a crack, not a fracture."

She began cutting the stems to size. "I guess I'll have to learn a whole new system of first-aid down here." Finished, she returned the knife to Allie. "I need three lengths of rope," she instructed. "Each long enough to wrap around her arm and tie securely." Carefully she placed the three trimmed stems around Mollow's arm, each spaced about a hundred and twenty degrees from the other two. Allie handed her the first rope, and she tied it snugly around the wrist. The second went up near the elbow, the last between the two.

"One more rope," she said. "It's the only thing we have that can be used for a sling. Mollow, I'd like to treat those wounds."

"There is the vial of blue tincture you can use to help seal the wounds." With her left hand, Mollow withdrew the parchment bag and passed it to her. "Just daub it around the edges of the wounds," she instructed. "That will suffice."

Allie stood up and took several steps to stretch his legs. He was unable to quell a yawn as he extended his arms to the limit. Finally he exhaled, a drawn-out sigh that signified an already-long day. But then, all days were long, Below.

Mollow got gingerly to her feet, and tested her mobility. At last she gave a little hiss of approval. "I can make it to the grove," she declared. For good measure, she added a staggered hiss that was her light laugh. "As long as I don't have to fly."

017: "Now you tell me."

Allie awoke screaming. The horrors that had occurred since the previous sleep had caught up with him in his dreams. Iskandar, swept away, disappearing into the cloud. Thadie, taken right from under his nose—and it did no good to tell himself there was nothing he could have done about that. The flight from the Deggs, and Mollow exhausting the energy she needed to maintain the form of the *thorga* and continue flying.

He did not recall sitting up, but on either side of him now were Thadie and Mollow. The latter's face nuzzled his neck, and her mouth cooed soothing words in her own language. He did not understand them, but he felt them. Thadie was checking him for wounds in case he had harmed himself in the throes of the dream. Magenta began to caress his cheek with hers.

After Allie came fully awake, he made another discovery. Thadie stank. He himself stank. And the water in the creek that flowed next to the grove barely covered their ankles.

Thadie caught him sniffing.

Mollow, also noticed. "There is an *azera*...a lake not far, and in the direction we wish to travel. You can bathe there. But you have no other clothing."

"So there are no malls Below," Allie said.

Mollow shot him a questioning look, which cleared up almost immediately. "Yes, there are many places where you may trade for clothing," she said. "But none nearby. And you have nothing to trade."

Allie dug into his pocket and pulled out the gold-bearing chunk of quartz. "What about this?" he asked. "Does it have value?"

Mollow examined it. "Yes," she concluded. "I think it might be enough." She handed it back to him. "But there is still the question of finding a place to trade."

"There is nothing at the gravesite?" Thadie asked.

"That is unknown to me," Mollow replied. "Whatever is there, is there, and we shall soon know. But first we should sleep more."

Allie nodded. "If I can."

~ * ~

Sometime later—Allie reckoned it at two hours—Mollow awoke them. After feeding themselves and Magenta—who now had a fondness for granola bars—they proceeded to the *azera*, the promised lake. It was not very large, perhaps a hundred yards across, and the lay of the land suggested it was not very deep. It appeared to be nothing more than a great puddle fed by the creek that flowed past the grove, and it had an outlet into another creek.

"I'd leave our clothes on," he told Thadie. "They could stand some water, too."

Thadie demurred and plucked at the hem of her tattered shift. "This is parchment," she reminded him. "It might well dissolve."

"You take it off and go first, then," he said, "and I'll look away. I think Maggie would like to hunt."

He moved off, and presently heard splashing. Moments later this was interrupted by a piercing scream. He started to head in that direction and saw Mollow rushing out into the water. Quickly she reached Thadie and pulled her out of the lake. She was hopping on one bare foot. To the other was attached some small creature. Allie thought it prudent to return his attention to the woegong, who was worrying at something under a rock. Presently he heard an, "Ow!" He did not look, but assumed the creature had been removed.

A long moment later, Thadie touched him on the shoulder. "Thanks for not looking," she said. "Your turn."

He stood up; his head began to ache again. "What was that?"

"Something with pincers. Mollow is building a fire."

Allie pointed at a nearby shrub. "Maggie is in there somewhere. She found something worthwhile."

With that, he dashed to the water's edge and dove in. The water was almost the same temperature as the air. Splashing about, he wished he had a bar of soap. He removed his shirt, swished it around in the water, and wrung it out before casting it ashore. Next came the slacks, which had need of repair, especially at the knees. He left his boots and underwear on and rubbed water all over his body. Something clamped onto his boot. He lifted that foot and found what Above might have been a large crayfish. Leaving the creature in place, he ambled ashore and had Mollow remove it before he dressed himself.

They sat around the fire munching on fragments of a bluish-white meat from the *pogarh*, as the creatures were called. Allie thought they tasted like and had the texture of crab; he wished they had some melted butter. Thadie ate tentatively at first, until she was satisfied with the taste.

It was Thadie who raised the question Allie realized he should have asked. "Mollow, couldn't you change shape to become, I don't know, some sort of vehicle with wheels? We could travel much faster that way."

The question puzzled Mollow. "I have never tried to do that. I do not know anyone who has tried." She tilted her head at Thadie, an acquired gesture. "Why would we want to do that?"

"Well...to travel around your settlement, for one thing. And to travel between settlements."

Mollow spoke as if the answer should have been obvious. "Settlements are small. All is within a short walking distance."

"It's a long walk to the next settlement, though," Allie said. "To the Lannars, for example. It's too bad you don't have any, you know, vehicles."

That surprised Mollow. "Oh, but we do."

Allie felt as if he had been swatted across the head with a board. He felt as if he should shake his head to clear it. His voice plunged a full octave. "What?"

Thadie dismissed this. "You don't even have any roads."

Again Mollow looked confused. "Why would we have need of them?"

"Mollow," Allie said carefully, "we have seen no signs of any vehicles." Thadie nodded emphatically, and he went on. "What are you talking about?"

"You would call them..." Mollow paused, thinking hard. "I do not know...perhaps to you they would be airfoils."

Allie's brow knit. "Airfoils."

"They pass over the land," Mollow explained. "We have no need to deface our land with roads."

"But we could have already been...," he sputtered. "We didn't have to..."

Mollow's tone saddened. "But this is not so, Allie. You said you wanted to walk around."

"But I-I thought you didn't...I mean..."

"We use them rarely," said Mollow. "Like you, we enjoy a walk."

"And…and the Lannar?"

"Yes."

"The Oiskins?"

"No," Mollow answered. "They are primitive."

"What about the Deggs? The ones who took Thadie."

"They have some vehicles. But they retain many primitive ways, including the hunt."

"Can we get an airfoil here?" Thadie asked, driving directly to the point.

"If I could let Gullaf or someone know what we needed," Mollow said. "But at this distance, no, I cannot. There is someone who could…but alas…"

"Iskandar," Allie sighed. His headache throbbed, almost like a migraine. But then it lessened and faded. "So what do we do?" he asked. "Just go on?"

"This is so."

"After a little more sleep," Thadie suggested.

~ * ~

One more day, as Allie thought of it: the period between sleeps. Soon enough it might well be over. A useful clue at the gravesite of Abner Perry was his ticket home. *Home*, he thought, stepping over rocks and the low-growing underbrush that thrived on this side of the *azera*, the lake. A day ago, as he measured time, he had not thought of Above as home. Now…

"You're deep in thought," Thadie said, picking her way around small shrubs. She snatched up a flower as she passed it. "Perhaps I had better watch, so you don't trip over anything."

Magenta crept up his arm until she could peer over his shoulder.

"Just random thoughts," he told her. "I do find it difficult to believe you would want to stay Below."

She arched a black eyebrow. "Really? Why is that, then?"

He looked away. "It's dangerous down here." His voice did not feel as if it were a part of him. "People get killed."

"It's dangerous everywhere, Allie. People get killed everywhere."

"Yes, but…"

A bit of mirth mixed into her sober expression. "You don't read the headlines much, do you?"

Still he would not meet her eyes. "I guess not."

A brook awaited their crossing. It was narrow enough to step over, but Thadie slipped on a loose rock and started to pitch forward. Allie started to reach for her, but Mollow, who was closer, caught her from behind with her good arm and eased her to the other bank. The terrain now ahead of them seemed level as it led up to the blue line of trees, now more readily distinguishable. There were obstacles to be rounded: outcrops of rock, and clumps of shrubbery, and even a herd of small brown and white animals that Above might have been called goats. But crossing this plain posed no overt threat to them.

Still, Mollow kept an eye on the air above them.

"Storms?" Allie asked, his voice shaking a little.

Mollow hissed negation. "The air is clear," she replied. "But we are out in the open, with no place of refuge for us, and there are *thorga* and other fliers. Most likely they will go for one of the *barzhals*...what you thought of a moment ago as goats."

"That's another thing I have Above," Allie said to Thadie. "Privacy."

"I know," Thadie said. "I too am accustomed to it. But I harbor no thoughts I wish to remain secret. It is the way here." She glanced his way. "Was there something you wanted to keep from Iskandar?"

"Don't. Just...don't, Thadie."

"I am sorry. It is difficult to know which topics to avoid, and which are sensitive, when one cannot read the index."

Despite himself, Allie almost laughed. "That is an odd way of putting it."

"But it is true," she persisted. "Secrecy enables people to fight, because they do not understand. It enables nations to go to war. There is no war here Below. Differences between cultures, between moieties, need not erupt into violence. In fact, I suspect violence such as what occurs Above would be unthinkable Below."

"There is slavery," Allie pointed out.

With questioning eyes Thadie turned to Mollow, who said, "Had we not intercepted those Deggs, as soon as possible your moiety would have come to take you back. This is understood, even by the Degg. Not every moiety is as protective, however."

"The Lannar is," Allie said.

"This is so."

A silence followed while they crossed flat terrain. Finally Thadie broke it. "I want to go shopping," she said, plucking at her parchment shift. "This thing is beginning to itch."

"Take it off, then," Allie said, without thinking.

To his surprise and utter consternation, she did so. Carefully she folded the parchment and handed it to Mollow to put into her pouch. She wore nothing underneath.

"I should desensitize myself to nakedness," she said. "It is the Alassal way, and I am of their moiety." She made a sound that was both peevish and casual. "Oh, Allie, it's all right. I am a part of this land. You may—"

"Over there," Mollow said, with sudden urgency. "Take to those shrubs and stay low, both of you."

They dashed away, with Mollow protectively behind them. "What is it?" Allie gasped.

"It is a *ulama*. You have no word for this. It is smaller than a *thorga*, but equally as dangerous. Stay low, between the shrubs. If it lands to pick at you, keep a shrub between you at all times. I will transform if I must."

Sprawled on the ground now, Allie looked up. This flier was jet black, as if it had evolved not caring whether it was seen. It passed overhead without even noticing them. It seemed to be headed for the *barzhal* herd. While he watched, the *ulama* dove down, and at the bottom of its stoop it snatched up an adult *barzhal* and flew off with it toward the forest and the mountains beyond. As it flew, its beak was already tearing at its prey, and Allie could hear its bleats of pain.

"Another reason for returning Above," he muttered. "As if I needed one."

Propped up on her elbows, Thadie lay beside him, an arm's length away. "Am I ugly?" she asked him. "Or disfigured?"

The question startled him. "What? No, no, not at all." He sighed. "I'm just not accustomed to...to..."

"Another reason for you to return Above, then," she said, disappointed. "Do you know why the Alassal wear clothing?" She gave him no chance to answer. "For protection. Mud splatters, climbing trees that have rough bark, that sort of thing. Allie, almost nobody wears clothes Below. When we first encountered Gullaf and Beterr, they were clothed only for the sake of our sensitivity. Unlike Above, there is no shame here."

"No body consciousness, you mean."

"So if you should look at me, you see a friend. Which is how I see you, clothed or not." She pushed herself up and glanced at Mollow. "Is it safe?"

"This is so," the Alassal said. "The *ulama* nest near the tops of the mountains. Probably this one has younglings to feed."

"Eyrie," Allie said. "And fledglings."

"Don't be pedantic," Thadie said.

Rising, she helped him up. He gave her a deliberate and slow once-over. "I'd brush that dirt off you," he said at last. "But that might be a bit too much and too soon."

"That's better." She gazed at the distant trees. "Five miles?" she asked him.

"It's hard…ah, make that 'difficult' to tell down here."

At the change of wording, she burst into laughter. It was the first time he had heard her reach the level of a guffaw.

"What is amusing?" Mollow asked, as they resumed their trek.

"I don't think I have the words," Thadie replied. "You'd better try reading us."

A moment later, she said, "Still I do not understand. You have simply exchanged one word for another."

"It's a human thing, Mollow," Allie said sagely. Thadie punched his arm.

018: A Promise Kept, Another Made

Again Allie's estimate of distance proved too little, this time by about half. Seen from up close, the forest looked foreboding. The gap in the tree line proved to be a collapse of the low escarpment that marked the boundary between the forest and the plains. Where Allie had expected some form of conifer, he found trees with broad blue leaves. The forest floor was littered with shed leaves that, oddly enough, had become chartreuse in dying. His ears caught a few light sounds; analogs of insects and birds, perhaps. Above him, leaves fluttered with the passing of some creature. All in all, he found the forest to be idyllic. That frightened him.

"There are no large creatures in here," Mollow assured him.

The gap became the entrance to a passageway that had seen some use in the past, although the few leaves that now lay upon it appeared to have been undisturbed. For as far as the eye could see, the path thus formed led up the gentle slope of a foothill, winding its way, with no sign of anything that might be a gravesite. Still, this was a path, and it had a purpose.

Disappointed, Allie shook his head. "This can't be right."

"It is what I was told," Mollow said. "I follow the legend. The site must be further up this trail."

"We are here," Thadie added. "We may as well check it out."

Allie sighed. "'Whose woods these are, I think I know,'" he murmured.

"What is that?" Mollow asked.

"Poem by Robert Frost," he replied. "You've probably never heard of him." Quietly he added, "And I do have promises to keep." He took a step forward, and another, and glanced back. "Coming?"

The forest sounds did not soften as they passed. Perhaps the denizens sensed no hostility, even though Magenta might have hunted some of them. The trail itself, softened by grass that grew out instead of up, reacted quietly to their footsteps. The glow from overhead cast few shadows, as it was already dark and deep, both in the trees and on the trail. Allie, lost in his own thoughts, said nothing. Only a few random whispers between Thadie and Mollow floated over the light breeze that wafted back down the trail.

They rounded a bend, only to find more trees. *Miles to go before I sleep*, Allie thought, and wondered whether Frost might have foreseen this. The slope began to level out, easing their ascent. They began to walk three abreast, like characters from a Dumas novel. Allie thought they should have been in a missing-man formation. He estimated they were now a mile into the forest. How much further? And at what point should they turn back around?

"I do not know," Mollow said, reading him.

"It is a pleasant time for a stroll," Thadie said.

Allie glanced at her and shook his head. A stroll had no purpose; he did. Anticipation of finding a way back up began to well inside him. He had no idea as to the identity of the clue, or even that there would be one. But he would go on. He would leave, and—if ever possible—forget what might have been. Somehow.

They rounded a sharp bend in the trail. Allie did not realize he had come to a stop. He was barely aware of the small building of cut yellow stone with a slightly gabled roof stood on the left side of the trail. He had no eyes for it, only for the stone bench in front of the building, and the dusky violet figure sitting on it.

"What kept you?" Iskandar asked.

Allie found the strength to move and took a step as she rose from the bench. "Traffic," he replied, hoarsely.

Their collision in the center of the trail was loud enough to startle the forest denizens into a brief silence. Allie and Iskandar were limpets clinging not to rocks, but to one another. Not a ray of light shone between them. Nor were their eyes dry.

Magenta poked her head up to regard both of them. Still coiled around Allie's arm, she laid her head and neck over Iskandar's shoulder.

Allie did not ask how, or what. Instead, he whispered into her ear. "I love you. I would like us to be mated."

"Then we are mated," she replied, her lips tickling his earlobe.

Neither Mollow nor Thadie spoke a word.

Finally Allie needed to catch a breath, and reluctantly loosened his embrace of Iskandar. She took a step back, a mild disbelief in her purple eyes. "I knew you would come," she said. "But when I 'sent' to you and you did not respond, I began to fear for you. I began to doubt."

An understanding fell into place as they turned to walk side by side toward the structure. "That was the headache I had. One of them, anyway," he added, with a glance back at Mollow. "Iskandar ...how?"

She stared straight ahead, remembering. "I could do nothing against the wind, except wait and wonder. And hope. When the cloud came apart and released me, I was over a lake. It was a fall I took. Had I been over land, I would be dead now. I struck the bottom. I was shocked to find myself still alive. I had no idea where you were, but I knew where you were going. And here I am, as are you."

They paused before the entrance to the structure. "Have you gone inside?" he asked her.

"There was no point in doing so," she answered. "If you came, we would enter together. If not, then nothing mattered to me." Suddenly she cried out. "Oh!" Whirling around, she threw her arms around Mollow. "I am so sorry," she whispered. "I was not thinking, my good friend. I am glad to see you as well."

Mollow hissed approval. "You had someone else on your mind. As you should."

"What...what happened to your arm?" she asked.

"I tried to fly."

The structure had neither door nor windows. Inside, darkness reigned. Allie caught a whiff of the musty smell of a mausoleum as he probed his way in the dark. Mollow found and touched a pad on the inner wall, and an illuminating panel in the ceiling began to glow. It revealed an oblong stone sarcophagus on a stand. The lid, also of stone, showed no sign of having been moved.

"It probably slides," Thadie offered.

"I've never opened a tomb before," Allie said. He shivered, though the interior was warm enough.

"There are etchings on the wall," Iskandar said.

"Do you see any words?" Allie asked. "Any instructions?"

"Or anything to identify who is in this sarcophagus," added Thadie.

"I do not know," Iskandar replied. "Come and look."

"Let's get this open first," Allie suggested.

Together they pushed the lid to one side, careful not to let it drop to the floor. Inside lay a skeleton with some flesh remaining.

There was nothing to identify it. The uniform it had been wearing had rotted away. The stench emanating from it made Allie's eyes water. Thadie turned her face aside, rubbing her nose as if the itch would not go away.

"There is only the body," Mollow said. "I see no other object in here. We should close the lid."

"But there has to be something," Allie moaned. "That is the legend. How did David leave Below, unless he found something here?"

"He may have taken it with him," Thadie suggested.

Unwillingly, Allie had to agree. His eyes continued to water from the smell. "All right, then, let's close this up and let the air clear."

"I am sorry," Iskandar told him. "I know you were hoping."

"I was so sure…" His haunted words failed him.

"May I speak?" she asked.

"Always. Please do not ask again, Iskandar. We are mated."

The corners of her purple lips curled up in a faint smile. "Perhaps you convinced yourself of an uncertainty, which made it seem real."

"Yeah, perhaps. Let's go outside and get some fresh…"

"Allie?" Thadie prodded, as his voice faded.

He moved to stand before an etching on the wall. There was just enough light for him to make out details. "This," he said, pointing with a shaking finger. "This is a *map!*"

They gathered around him. He jabbed a finger here and there. "See? That's the river, the Fiumna. Here's the lake where Thadie caught the *pogarh*. Here's that marmot…that, that narnot, the sea, Iskandar, where the Degg live."

"To be precise, the *pogarh* caught me," Thadie said.

She was still naked, and he found himself starting to take her appearance in stride. "Nice bait," he said, and turned back to the map.

"Gullaf thinks so," Mollow said.

Gasping, Thadie whirled to her. "He said that? Did he really say that?"

Mollow tapped a finger to the side of her head.

Allie ignored them. "And here is the forest, the trail, and here's where we are. But what's this, a trail…?"

On the wall, the trail snaked upwards between the sea and the mountains. Near the point where the wall met the ceiling, a spot of ochre was beginning to fade. It was the word scratched into the stone beside it that captured Allie's full attention.

What seemed an eternity later, he whispered the word. "Here."

Thadie temporized. "It could indicate the location of great danger," she said.

"What is that below it?" Mollow asked, pointing.

"OI," Thadie said. "Probably for Oiskin. They would be a danger to the unwary.

"No," Allie said dully. "No. That's not an O. That's a D. David Innis. He was here, and he found this. Or he etched it,"

"Either way, then, that must represent the way out," Thadie said.

Allie's voice grew sadder. "And the way in." He shook his head slowly and spoke now with hard decision. "That opening has to be plugged."

Thadie gently cleared her throat. "I thought you were leaving."

He looked long and longingly at Iskandar. "Never," he said.

Iskandar stepped forward and placed her hands on his shoulders. "We are mated, as we declared to one another. You are now of the Lannar moiety. But there is more, Allie. You are of my hearth." She gave a soft look to Mollow, who had brought Allie to her. "And you, my friend. You have already drunk my water—"

"Our water, then," Allie amended.

"Yes. Our water. That still entitles you to our protection," here she shifted her gaze to Allie, who inclined his head in assent, "and also to our comfort."

"If we can get back to the moieties," Thadie groused.

Iskandar looked at her wonderingly. "But I have already arranged this. Did I not say?"

Thadie sputtered. "You said not." She made a face. "*God in die hemel*, I'm bloody talking like you now."

"I have 'sent' to Bofiri for an airfoil," she said, touching her head for additional explanation. She stepped outside onto the trail, the others following, and keened an ear. "She will arrive presently."

"How…?" Allie asked. "Mollow was unable to reach the Alassal moiety."

"We are not all the same, Allie," Iskandar said, as if he needed a gentle reminder.

Thadie studied each of them in turn. "Yes," she said, and touched her head and her heart. "We are."

About the Author

The author is a retired U. S. Army translator with a hogshead of novels, novellas, and short stories in his resume. He writes the Bombay Sapphire superheroine series for Pro Se Press and the Yoelin Thibbony Child Rescue series for Nomadic Delirium Press. He is also the Managing Editor of Hiraeth Publishing.

He lives in the Southwest with Coda and Laika—two husky-lab mixes that keep him in shape.

More Books from
WolfSinger Publications

Mars in Carnage – William Paul Lazarus

Humanity's dream of colonizing Mars quickly becomes a fight for survival. Mission director Lt Col. John Hathaway sends astronauts Aadya "Kate" Khatun and Hamza "Arti" Artsruni to explore and establish a foothold on the Red Planet. One astronaut is killed, during what appears to be an alien attack; the other makes a solo, dangerous return to a hero's welcome on Earth.

Over a century later a Martian colony has firmly established—the underground city of Katarti, Cecil Townley, a tour guide for visitors to Mars is captured by a band of terrorists trying to end what they believe are horrible governmental actions on Mars. Hiding in underground tunnels, they begin their attack with Townley forced to be their guide. Their actions introduce him to a world he never knew existed, far from the innocent tale he had been telling newcomers for years.

Cowboy Up – edited by Carol Hightshoe

Cowboy Up gathers stories that celebrate the timeless tradition of rodeo. The dust, the grit, the glory—it's all here.

From the echoes of the past to the rodeo arenas of today, these stories will take you on a wild ride through the highs and lows of rodeo life. You'll share in their triumphs and their heartbreaks. From the unbreakable bond between rider and horse to the courage it takes to get back in the saddle after a fall, this anthology is a tribute to the spirit that keeps rodeo alive.

But this book isn't just about telling stories. It's about giving back. Eighty-Five percent of proceeds from Cowboy Up will be donated to the Justin Cowboy Crisis Fund, a non-profit organization dedicated to helping injured rodeo athletes get back on their feet. Your purchase helps support those who risk it all in the arena, offering them a lifeline when they need it most.

So saddle up. Dive into these tales of resilience, heart, and the cowboy way. With every story, you're not just reading about rodeo—you're helping to keep its spirit alive.

Homefall Search — Dana Bell

Charged with finding the best place for a new Homefall, Jehna Talon searched on Saris, a world located in the Tashiti Nebula. Along with her Arial shapeshifter companions, she goes into the Ghost Mountains to find a specific valley, only to become trapped during a storm and encounters a native dragon.

With local rancher Harrison Talbot she negotiates the price for the land. Brides, for him and his hands. As her uncle taught her, there's always a need to be filled. Traveling to Aris and with the help of a local contact, she finds women willing to brave the frontiers of space.

Returning to Ronia, home of the Talons, she learns opposition from the other clan leaders may stop the dream she had of becoming a clan leader. They argue there are too few Rovers, and she'll never succeed.

Could they be right, despite her already finding the ideal location?

The Dragon's Hoard 3 — edited by Carol Hightshoe

In this anthology, twenty-six authors weave enchanting stories of dragons—from the fierce and fire-breathing to the wise and benevolent. Enter a treasure trove of tales where dragons reign supreme and hoards are more than mere gold.

Discover hidden gems of wisdom and magic within these lairs. Feast on tales that shimmer with magic, adventure, and the timeless allure of dragons. Explore the myriad treasures dragons hold dear and the legends that surround them.

From heartwarming tales of friendship and loyalty to thrilling adventures filled with danger and magic, these tales offer something for every dragon lover. Whether they are guardians of treasure, seekers of knowledge, or forces of nature: the dragons in this collection will ignite your imagination.

The Dragon's Hoard 2 — edited by Carol Hightshoe

Welcome to realms where dragons reign, treasures abound, and every adventure leads to magic. Explore stories that spark the imagination and might just awaken the dragon within. Are you brave enough to face the dragon and claim your prize?

From the unyielding grip of ancient magics to the cunning of those who seek dragons, their treasure or both—each story weaves a rich tapestry of magic and lore.

Whether it's a battle for survival, the forging of an unlikely alliance, or a humorous twist on hoarding habits, our authors invite you to delve into realms where dragons not only hoard gold but also secrets, spells, and sometimes, even friendships. After all, in the world of dragons, not all treasures are silver and gold—some are stories waiting to be told.

The Hounds of Ardagh – Laura J Underwood

Ginny Ni Cooley never desired more than the simple life she had, living in Tamhasg Wood and using her magic to occasionally assist the folk of Conorscroft while putting up with the machinations of the ghost of her former mentor Manus MacGreeley. But her peace is shattered one night with the arrival of a lad who is fleeing a pack of red-gold hounds led by a hound-shaped demon known as Nidubh.

So much for peace and solitude. By rescuing Fafne MacArdagh, Ginny becomes wrapped in the fabric of an intrigue involving a family feud, a traitorous son, and a blood mage named Edain who is determined to keep her soul. It is she who cast a spell on Fafne's family and household and transformed the MacArdaghs into hounds.

Ginny gives Fafne her word to take him to Caer Keltora so they can report the matter to the Council of Mageborn. But Edain is determined to keep her secret and her soul intact and moves to thwart Ginny at every turn.

For Ginny Ni Cooley who has faced many bogies, dealing with a demon, a bloodmage and the Dark Lord of Annwn will be no easy task. But she will do what she must to undo Edain's spells. If not, Manus' soul will become part of Arawn's Cauldron of Doom. Ginny will become a demon's feast, and poor Fafne will join the Hounds of Ardagh.

Wee Folk and Wise: A Fairies Anthology
— edited by Deby Fredericks

All over the world, fairy tales are told.
There are big fairies and little fairies.
Ugly fairies and pretty fairies.
Wise fairies and silly fairies.
Sweet fairies and scary fairies.

Seventeen authors share their own fantastic fairy tales in this magical collection. What kind of fairy will you meet here?

Infinity *— Ted Pennella*

In the distant future, when peace between humanity and the artificial intelligences their ancestors created has been settled, Conrad Conner tries to live a quiet and unassuming life in orbit about Jupiter on the city-station Socrates' Odyssey. When Conner's attempt to create a prototypical communication artificial for use by the Sol-Humana Confederation's Stellar Fleet gets derailed by the attempted murder of the very artificial he's created, his life spirals into a mad flight back to Earth to try and save at least his sister's children, if not his sister herself. Past failures and heartaches resurface as seemingly unconnected dots become a plot by the First Admiral to steal not just power over the Confederation, but a secret Conner holds within himself.

A secret not even Conner knows about.

Flatlanders *- Mike Sherer*

Young theoretical physicist Mickey Haiku has fallen into Eden's trap. She is a much smarter scientist who is intent on saving her own dimension by destroying his. Unbeknownst to either, beings from several yet higher dimensions have their own strategies. This sends the mixed-up pawns off on a wild odyssey through a dozen weird, twisted dimensions. As if this hyper-dimensional odyssey isn't challenging enough for Mickey, he has the additional difficulty of embarking on this whacko tour as a (pregnant!) female. Which means Eden is stuck in Mickey's body. The two are soon forced to cooperate since each holds the other's body hostage.

The strangest relationship this side of the 11th dimension

develops between the two.

Fires of Rapiveshta: Book Three: A Familiar's Tale
— Verna Mckinnon

With Obsydia's chaos growing and more kingdoms falling under her control, Runa, Mellypip and their friends scramble to find a way to stop her from discarding her mortal form and claiming their world in the name of her Eternal Father Ahridum and plunging it into a never-ending age of darkness and evil.

The dragons of Rapiveshta are awakened from their long slumber by Obsydia's attempt to steal the egg that holds the unborn dragon who will become the next leader of the dragon clans. The egg is given to Runa's grandfather to protect it. When it hatches, Mellypip finds himself bonded to the baby dragon as her guardian.

As Obsydia reaches the climax of the ritual that will burn away her mortality, Runa, Opaline and Panthara find themselves captured to be used as sacrifices. Will the Gate of Souls claim Runa and Mellypip as the Winged Fey have foreseen? Or will the Fires of Rapiveshta and those chosen to be the Scions of Light be able to save them and their world.

And more – check out our books at
www.wolfsingerpubs.com